Unconsciously, Poppy's hands went to her belly, where the burgeoning swell of her abdomen had been cleverly disguised as much as possible by her stylist.

She couldn't blame the baby in her womb for this scramble to get married. She could only blame herself and the monumental weakness she'd displayed when faced with the world's most notorious playboy, who had gone from being a crown prince, to a king, only to fall from grace and become a mere prince again.

The worst of it was, she knew that even if she went back in time and was faced with the same scenario again, she couldn't truly say she would have behaved any differently...

A spectacular new royal duet
from Harlequin Presents author Abby Green!

Royal House of Sadat

A crown in crisis...

Royal scandal has rocked the unshakable house of Sadat. When news of the late king's affair shocks the nation, his heir, King Caius, is forced to abdicate. Now his sister, Princess Cassie, must take up the mantle.

Their futures were once etched in stone. But with the line of succession altered forever, can Sadat's royal siblings take destiny into their own hands?

Find out in
Bodyguard's Royal Temptation

Desperate for one final taste of freedom before her coronation, Crown Princess Cassie escapes to the shimmering shores of Greece. Her brother's best friend, Ares, security tycoon and now her personal bodyguard, isn't far behind her! She might resent his presence, but can't deny the irresistible magnetism between them...

Unmasking His Pregnant Queen

Former King Caius is embracing life as a playboy tycoon. Until a red-hot rendezvous with a masked stranger in Paris has royal consequences that threaten his newfound bachelor status! If the shock of first fatherhood wasn't enough, he discovers his anonymous beauty is his once betrothed, Crown Princess Poppy of Valdere!

Both available now!

UNMASKING HIS PREGNANT QUEEN

ABBY GREEN

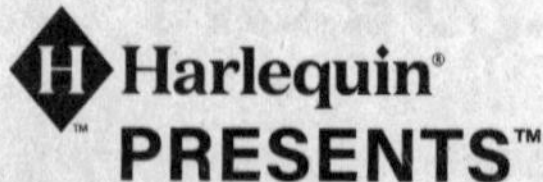

Recycling programs for this product may not exist in your area.

ISBN-13: 978-1-335-21385-3

Unmasking His Pregnant Queen

For questions and comments about the quality of this book, please contact us at CustomerService@Harlequin.com.

Harlequin Enterprises ULC
22 Adelaide St. West, 41st Floor
Toronto, Ontario M5H 4E3, Canada
www.Harlequin.com

HarperCollins Publishers
Macken House, 39/40 Mayor Street Upper,
Dublin 1, D01 C9W8, Ireland
www.HarperCollins.com

Printed in Lithuania

Irish author **Abby Green** ended a very glamorous career in film and TV—which really consisted of a lot of standing in the rain outside actors' trailers—to pursue her love of romance. After she'd bombarded Harlequin with manuscripts, they kindly accepted one, and an author was born. She lives in Dublin, Ireland, and loves any excuse for distraction. Visit abby-green.com or email abbygreenauthor@gmail.com.

Books by Abby Green

Harlequin Presents

Heir for His Empire
"I Do" for Revenge
Rush to the Altar
Billion-Dollar Baby Shock
Bride of Betrayal

Princess Brides for Royal Brothers

Mistaken as His Royal Bride

Hot Winter Escapes

Claimed by the Crown Prince

Brazilian Billionaire Brothers

The Heir Dilemma
On His Bride's Terms

Royal House of Sadat

Bodyguard's Royal Temptation

Visit the Author Profile page
at Harlequin.com for more titles.

CHAPTER ONE

Wedding Day

It was Poppy's wedding day and she felt a self-indulgent moment of wishing she knew what it felt like to be ecstatic like most normal brides. But she wasn't a normal bride. She was a royal bride, a crown princess, of the House of Valdun, of Valdere. So, for her, the norms had been subverted from birth, in more ways than one.

For one thing, her marriage had always been destined to be arranged, or strategic, and for another, because she'd been born a girl and not a boy, she had no choice but to marry in order to become queen of her small but stunning Alpine monarchy, Valdere.

Her father had set that in stone, and it had become more and more set in stone when he'd failed to sire any more children than Poppy, or, more crucially, have a much coveted son. When his first wife, Poppy's mother—a glamorous American actress and model—hadn't obliged, he'd divorced her and married again. And again. And again. Each marriage ending in acrimony and no more children.

It had been the most egregious of double standards

because a boy would've been crowned king on the death of the late king, a year ago, but because Poppy was a woman, the law had decreed she must marry before being crowned queen.

It had been a final insult and humiliation from a father who had never seen her as anything but a sign of his failure to have the right heir. His last words to her had been, *You will not be queen until you have a king by your side.* Poppy had begged him to reconsider but he'd refused.

And so, on his death, Poppy had hidden her humiliation and hurt, grieved publicly for a man who had never really loved her and she'd spent the last year preparing herself for a role she would've been infinitely better prepared for if she'd been a man.

Thankfully the work of phasing out her father's old counsel had proved relatively seamless as they were of retirement age and happy to step aside—maybe they'd been worn out by her father's intransigence too.

Part of her father's legacy had been his reluctance to give Poppy too much exposure, not wanting to admit defeat that she was his only heir. And so, unlike most royals who were trotted out at every opportunity, she'd managed to stay a relatively obscure figure on the world's stage.

One source of solace was the people of Valdere who, in the past year, had come to know their crown princess in a way her father had never encouraged while he was alive and they'd taken her to their hearts, because she was intent on ushering in change and breathing new life into a country with a young population who were eager to move on from the old-fashioned ways of people like her father.

But one thing she'd had no control over was the fact that she still had to marry to become queen. So here she was. Not ecstatic. The lavish wedding ceremony today would also incorporate the necessary rites for her coronation.

And that of her husband-to-be, Prince Caius of Sadat Sur Mer, a small island monarchy in the Mediterranean. He was to become her king consort.

If he could be bothered to turn up. To say he was a reluctant participant in this wedding was the understatement of the year.

There was a discreet knock on the door to her bedroom and she said, 'Come in.'

Poppy fought back the rising sense of panic when she saw one of her most trusted aides enter. She'd gone to university in America with Stephen and he'd generously agreed to work with her, helping her haul her beloved country into the modern age. He and his partner, Joel, were close friends.

In answer to the question she hadn't even asked, he just shook his head but said quickly, 'He *is* in the air, but not landed yet.'

Poppy looked back at her reflection in the mirror, barely taking in the high-necked antique cream lace dress, and asked, 'Are we even sure he's on the plane?'

The wedding was to take place in an hour. Even if Caius was on the plane, he'd barely make it to the cathedral on time. The old wound of rejection stung. It tugged on the deepest, most secret part of Poppy where she yearned to have a real relationship—she'd never be so naive as to ask for love, but was it too much to hope for companionship, respect, kindness? Maybe even passion?

She had a flashback to a night many weeks before when she'd learnt what passion was for the first time. She'd never expected it to be so earthy, heart-thumpingly exciting or transcendent. The fact that it had happened so unexpectedly and with the worst possible man had taught her a valuable lesson that good sex had nothing to do with emotion.

She looked at Stephen. 'This is all my fault. If I hadn't gone to Paris to see what he was really like, we wouldn't be in this situation now.'

'You'd still be in this situation,' Stephen pointed out softly. 'Just with someone else and maybe the devil you know is not such a bad thing.'

Poppy shivered at that. *Devil.* Caius had certainly appealed to the most devilish part of her when she'd met him in Paris sixteen weeks ago. He'd still been king of his own monarchy at that point. It hadn't yet become public knowledge that his father, the late king of Sadat Sur Mer, hadn't actually been Caius's biological father.

But before Paris and then the abdication, there had been the talks to dicusss a marriage. They'd had a conference phone call and before Caius had known she was connected and waiting to talk to him, she'd heard him speaking with his aides. 'She's a social hermit, I've never once met her at an event. In the formal photo we were sent she looks about ten years older than she is and in need of a serious makeover. Any other picture we unearthed isn't much better. And what kind of a name is Poppy for a queen? She's not an art student.'

Another male voice, sounding amused, had said, 'So if she's not your type, why bother?'

Caius had sounded grim. 'Because she doesn't need to be my type. Valdere is strategically important, positioned as it is in the centre of Europe. It has great potential to become a financial banking hub, on a par with Switzerland. And we just need each other to provide heirs and spares for both our monarchies to keep the royal bloodlines intact. If we marry, I'll be discreet but I won't give up my freedom.'

'What about her?'

'She can do as she pleases, as long as she's discreet too.'

At this point, on the other end of the line, Poppy had been aghast, her mouth wide open. It wasn't as if she didn't know how royal marriages worked, but she'd never heard it laid out with such brutal cynicism.

She'd been tempted to put the phone down on such arrogance but Stephen, who'd been there, had shaken his head silently, cautioning her not to be too hasty. She'd swallowed her hurt pride and had let him make it known that they were now ready to take the call.

Caius's tone had changed of course. To prince charming. But at least she hadn't been fooled. They'd been civil and she'd agreed to seriously consider an engagement. At one point she'd said, 'You don't seem to think it's necessary to meet?'

There'd been a pause on the other end of the phone and then Caius had sounded more like the man she'd heard at the start. 'Look, we both know how these things work. It's not as if we have much room to manoeuvre. We'll do what's required and get on with our lives. Come together for formal occasions when necessary. But as far as I'm concerned you and our…children can still live in Valdere while I remain primarily in Sadat Sur Mer. Once we're married any interest will die down anyway.'

Poppy had been tempted to retort that interest would die down a lot quicker once he stopped courting attention and sleeping with every supermodel the world had ever known.

She'd put the phone down finally and looked at Stephen and shaken her head. 'No way. He is not going to be the father of my children and live a separate life. I will not put them through what I experienced, a life of painful rejection and neglect from their father.'

'Don't be too quick to judge,' her advisor had counselled. 'I don't need to remind you that you need to marry to become queen, and you can't bring in any substantial changes until you are queen. Maybe a marriage that allows you to get on with matters of the state with minimal interference isn't such a bad thing.'

He'd then pointed out, 'As far as choice goes, you've already ruled out many of the contenders.'

Poppy had grimaced. It wasn't that she was being difficult about choosing a potential king consort, but the available bachelor royals hadn't been appealing enough to entice her. They were either too conservative, or too partial to drugs, or one in particular who was looking for a new monarchy to feather his nest after being summarily cast out of his own for rumoured sex offences. No. Way.

So, actually, Caius Mansur de Roche, even with his playboy reputation, wasn't the worst choice, and Stephen had a point. If he was willing to leave her alone to be queen of her country, maybe it wouldn't be such a bad thing.

Poppy had had to concede that wanting to have a king consort who would also be a fully committed and loving father to his children might well be hoping for too much. After all, they would have her and she would ensure that they never felt unloved or unwanted. She'd already put plans in place to change the rules of inheritance so that if her firstborn was a girl, she could become queen.

Stephen had continued wryly, 'He had a point about that picture of you.'

Poppy had winced. The photo in question had been commissioned by her father before he'd died and she'd been styled and made up by a team who'd made her look as if she were from another era. Older than her years and unbelievably staid.

Thankfully, since her father's death, she'd been able to hire her own team and had undergone something of a makeover. She'd always loved fashion and was enjoying experimenting with different looks.

Then Stephen had said, 'You've been invited to that masked ball in Paris. Caius will undoubtedly be there—it's in aid of one of his charities. You should go, see him in person and then decide if you want to shut the door.'

Well, she had gone to that ball and he had been there and to say it had changed her life was an understatement.

Stephen's phone rang now, scattering Poppy's thoughts. He answered it and she went over to the French doors in her bedroom that opened out onto a terrace overlooking the small but impressive city of Valdere—it was a fairy-tale image with the mountains behind the palace and the city spread along the shores of a sparkling lake.

There was an island in the middle of the lake that housed another royal residence. A romantic chateau built by one of Poppy's ancestors for one of his mistresses. In plain sight of the main palace. A timely reminder of the reality of a royal marriage.

A lot of the buildings dated back to the 1800s when the main industry had been textiles and wealthy merchants had been influenced by their travels to places like Morocco and Asia.

Poppy could see the spire of the medieval cathedral soaring over the terracotta rooftops but she wasn't seeing the view. Her mind was inwards. Unconsciously her hands went to her belly, where the burgeoning swell of her abdomen had been cleverly disguised as much as possible by her new stylist.

She couldn't blame the baby in her womb for this scramble to get married. She could only blame herself and the monumental weakness she'd displayed when faced with the world's most notorious playboy king who had since fallen from grace and become a mere prince again.

The worst of it was, she knew that even if she went back in time, and was faced with the same scenario again, she couldn't truly say she would have behaved any differently…

Paris, four months ago

It wasn't hard to spot the man Poppy was looking for in the crowd. Not only did he stand head and shoulders above most of the other guests at this masked ball, he carried himself with the authority and innate privilege that came with being more than a mere mortal. A king. King Caius Mansur de Roche, to be specific.

Even with the black mask that covered half his face he was recognisable. The high forehead. Dark slashing brows. Thick dark hair, just this side of messy. Strong jaw covered with short dark beard. The formidable physique more suited to an athlete than a pampered member of the royal elite.

As crown prince, Caius had blazed a trail through the world's most glittering hot spots and had never been without a beautiful woman on his arm. They'd rarely lasted longer than one or two public outings though. He was known to be an inveterate playboy and finding him here in the thick of this glittering exclusive masked ball only confirmed what Poppy already knew. He was in no real hurry to settle down—because he didn't have to, like her, even if her country was *strategically attractive*.

She frowned under her own mask now. She'd come here to see him up close. To try and get the measure of the man who she'd spoken to on the phone only a few days ago to discuss the suitability of a marriage match. *After* overhearing his unflattering opinion of her. That she looked ten years older than she was and needed a serious makeover.

She hated to admit it but part of her coming here had to do with her piqued feminine pride that he thought her so inconsequential. It had stung somewhere very vulnerable. Thanks to her new stylist, she could now come to a party like this in Paris and not feel like a wallflower.

But she was in disguise because she wanted the luxury of observing King Caius in his natural environment to see just how debauched he really was.

So she'd coloured her distinctive auburn hair with a wash-out colour of dark brown and was wearing dark contact lenses to hide her green eyes. Not that Caius would even have recognised her anyway. *Not his type.* She didn't like to admit it but maybe a part of her was still afraid of rejection even if he saw the new, improved version of herself.

Caius, was, after all, one of the most photographed and coveted bachelors on the planet. Aside from being a king, and somehow in spite of his relentless socialising, he was also a renowned financier. Respected the world over for his acumen. He'd built up a fortune to rival the one he'd inherited on his coronation day.

But there was something about his insanely good looks that had caught at Poppy whenever she'd looked him up online, even as his social whirl made her wonder what on earth he was chasing.

He was so masculine, in a way that no royal playboy should be. And, even though he was always smiling and charming and undeniably sexy, she'd sensed that there was something more underneath the devil-may-care surface. Something a bit…bleak that she recognised. To think for a second that they might be kindred spirits? Deluded.

She snorted a little to herself from her vantage point at the side of the ballroom. She knew what was underneath the charm. A deep and toxic seam of cynicism. And arrogance.

For a second she was almost tempted to turn tail and go back to Valdere, but then she thought of the effort she'd put in to come here, and of convincing Stephen that she really didn't even need her security to shadow her at the party because she'd be in disguise…and before she could change her mind, she helped herself to a glass of champagne, took a breath and dived into the crowd and made her way to where the man was holding court in the centre of the room, surrounded by adoring acolytes.

'And then…' Caius delayed his punchline, letting the tension build. He looked at the faces around him, tilted towards him, eyes shining, mouths open. Men vying for his attention, women vying for *him*, lust in their eyes and not just for the physical but for so much more. For status…as his queen.

As Caius drew the moment out, he imagined just stepping back, into the crowd and melting away. Leaving them all looking at an empty space. Because he was empty inside. Hollow. And he felt it in this moment. These people couldn't care less about him. He couldn't care less about them.

Was this it? Even once he acquired a queen and had heirs, would he still feel this…*lonely*?

At the last second, just when he noticed a couple of people look at each other as if to ask if he'd lost it, Caius delivered the punchline, some inanity, that wasn't all that funny, and yet they squealed and guffawed with laughter.

'You're *awful*, Caius…or must we address you as King Caius now?' said a voice close to his ear with an accompanying hand on his arm, squeezing possessively. He looked to his side to see a woman he recognised, even under her mask. He'd slept with her once and, ever since, she'd been angling to get back into his bed, but now his insides turned over at her cloying perfume and he shook his arm free.

'Excuse me, there's someone I need to speak with.'

He saw the flash of displeasure in her eyes as he turned away and it only compounded a growing sense of desperation. He could leave this party, he knew that. But to do what? Go where?

Go back to Sadat and concentrate on matters of the state? suggested a little voice. Yes, of course he could do that. Should do that. But somehow the thought of his serene island home, with its pretty main town, sparkling marina and rocky shores, didn't even entice.

He also had the pressing matter of a queen to consider, the unsavoury prospect of which was non-negotiable. His team had found him—in their eyes—a perfect candidate, and on paper she was. Young, single, a crown princess in possession of a monarchy in a strategically attractive part of Europe. Central to everything and full of economic potential. She was also a crown princess in desperate need of a king, as she couldn't become sovereign until she married—a fact his team had unearthed.

She, however, had little personal appeal for Caius and even though he knew this was a good recipe for a harmonious marriage—the last thing he wanted was a repeat of his parents' histrionics—he felt reluctant.

It was as if, since he'd become king, he'd become more and more aware that *this was it.* He was now king and yet on his coronation day he hadn't felt any great sense of…coming home. Or that he was finally in his rightful place. He'd always thought that once he was king, he'd feel more of a sense of belonging but, if anything, as he'd looked out over the crowd of people, he'd felt even more alienated. Worse, he'd felt a void inside him.

Caius didn't remember his father ever being remotely warm or affectionate. He'd always looked at Caius with a strange expression, almost suspiciously. And he'd been embroiled in the toxic relationship with Caius's mother. Their arguments had been epic and volcanic. The toxicity had spread throughout the palace, infecting everything.

Caius had a younger sister, Cassie, and he'd done his best to shield her from it, but suspected he hadn't been very effective. He'd escaped as soon as he could, but wherever he'd gone he'd brought a circus of rabid press to document his every move. It had become easier to give in to it than to avoid it, and he'd found that it had become a seductive smokescreen to hide the fact that he'd been born purely as a means to an end. To be an heir. It was like an invisible tattoo on his skin. *Unwanted and unloved. But useful for his bloodline.*

The fact that his usual social whirl wasn't distracting him was not a good sign. His uncharacteristic introspection mocked him. In this world who grew up with adoring parents? It was an urban myth. Laughable. You grew up and survived and then you did the same to the next generation and maybe hoped to do a little bit better. Especially if you were royalty.

Caius spotted a waiter weaving through the crowd with a tray of glasses of sparkling wine. He plucked a full glass from the tray and turned to make his way to somewhere he could try and shake himself out of this funk.

But just as he was about to take a step forward he collided with something. He heard a shocked gasp and looked down. It wasn't something, it was *someone*. A woman, who was looking up at him. A few inches shorter than him. A black lace mask covered the top half of her face but he could see a straight nose, delicately defined jaw and a mouth that made him look again. Full and sensual.

Dark eyes under the mask. Dark lustrous hair pulled back into a careless bun. But when he looked down further his heart stopped and then started to gallop. She was wearing a tuxedo suit. Like the men. Slim-fitting straight trousers. White shirt. Black jacket. But no tie.

Her shirt was open at the neck, a bow tie artfully dangling open. From here, Caius could see the shadowy cleft of generous cleavage.

It was so surprising to see a woman dressed like this that Caius took a step back. She looked shocked too. And it was only then that Caius noticed that she was holding a glass and that it was now empty and the contents all over the chest of her shirt, spreading in a wet stain.

Along with the contents of his own glass.

'I'm so sorry,' he said, realising what had happened and why she was looking so shocked. 'I didn't see you there.'

She seemed to be recovering, pulling her shirt out a little, which only made it clear that she was drenched.

'Here, give me your glass.'

She looked up and handed her glass to Caius. He noticed that she had a little dimple in her chin. It rang a faint bell in his head. He must know her from somewhere as this social milieu was a relatively small one but he knew that it wasn't an intimate connection.

He wasn't that rampant. The press had been wildly exaggerating his exploits for so long now that he hardly noticed. He handed the glasses to a passing waiter and when his discreet security detail asked if he could be of assistance, Caius said, 'Find us a private space, please, and some hotel staff.'

The woman protested, 'It's fine, don't worry. It's not that bad.' He noticed her voice had a pleasingly low timbre. Also, that anyone else in this situation would be raising hell right about now.

Things were already in motion. When Caius spoke, people jumped. Within seconds, they were being ushered out of the ballroom and down a corridor and into an empty reception room.

Once in the room, the woman looked at him and he couldn't help but notice the way the wet fabric of her shirt was clinging to her breasts. They looked high and full, and he could see the dip of her waist and long legs. She had a very classic womanly elegance underpinned by a sensuality that sent a spike of awareness into his blood.

She said, 'This really isn't necessary, I can sort myself out.'

It had been a long time since a woman had had such an immediate effect on him. Feeling a compelling urge not to let her out of his sight, Caius said, 'Absolutely not, I did this and I'll make sure you have that shirt washed and returned as soon as possible.'

Poppy felt the force of that deep sexy voice in her body, where she was still tingling from the volt of electricity generated when he'd collided with her, upending her full glass of champagne all over herself. And his own.

She *had* been standing right behind him, hoping to overhear some conversation, get a feel for what he was like in his natural habitat. She hadn't expected him to turn and walk right into her.

He'd been like a steel wall. A solid mass of muscle. Up close he was bigger and broader than she'd imagined he would be. He'd made her feel positively petite and she wasn't that small.

He obviously had no clue who she was. Nor did anyone else. She liked being incognito.

She arched a brow over the mask. A small smile played around her mouth. 'How do you plan on doing that?'

He'd started taking off his jacket before she'd fully registered what was happening and, after dropping it onto a nearby chair, he undid his bow tie and started to undo his shirt, saying, 'I'll give you my shirt and yours can be taken to be dried, or replaced.'

Poppy opened her mouth to protest but nothing came out as his shirt was opening now and revealing his chest. His very defined and hard-muscled chest. With dark hair covering his pectorals. For some reason she hadn't expected him to be so…unashamedly masculine. She'd expected him to be softer, more metrosexual.

He was giving her the shirt off his back. Literally. Totally bemused, Poppy took the shirt from the now half-naked Caius Mansur.

He said, 'I'll give you some privacy.' He walked away towards a window, his back to her, and she finally forced her feet to move, over to the opposite corner. She pulled off the jacket and undid the buttons on the sodden shirt. She pulled it off, and cast a quick glance over her shoulder.

Caius was still facing towards the window, hands in his pockets, but she was momentarily distracted by his naked back. Broad and smooth. Not an inch of spare olive-toned skin. Wide shoulders. Strong arms. Narrow waist. And down…to where he filled out his tuxedo trousers in a way that was frankly pornographic.

And then she looked up. She could see the hard lines of his face. His sheer beauty. Perfect bone structure and a strong jaw. A blade of a nose and slashing dark brows. And that mouth…the mouth that gave him away as a sybarite.

Those distinctive piercing blue eyes, visible even through the mask he still wore. Looking at her through the reflection.

Her breath stopped. Her skin prickled. He was watching her. She should be outraged. But it was hard to feel outraged when she was looking at him too. And when her blood seemed to have turned hot and molten and slow. Like lava.

Her heart thudded against her breastbone. No man had ever affected her so viscerally before and she was surprised.

She liked to think she was discerning enough not to fall at his feet in a swoon like the women who'd just been gazing at him with open adoration back in that ballroom. But here she was with suspiciously weak knees.

She blamed her sexual innocence for her reaction. Even though she'd gone to university in the United States, her constant security detail, albeit discreet, had scuppered any chance of a relationship. But that hadn't been the only deterrent. The lifelong wound of being so comprehensively rejected by her father had also made her wary of allowing anyone too close.

Not that Caius Mansur would ever find out how innocent she was. Or her vulnerabilities. Everything she'd seen so far only confirmed what she already knew. He was a playboy. He'd had her taking off her clothes within minutes of meeting her! *Not his fault,* pointed out a voice. Poppy ignored it, feeling a strong need to keep Caius at a distance.

She turned away from that provocative reflection and pulled on his shirt and suddenly that compulsion to keep her distance dissolved like snow on a hot stone. The material still held his warmth, and, worse, his smell. It wasn't overpowering and overtly masculine. It was subtle and evocative. Not what she'd expected. It made her close her eyes and think of the wild sea, warm earth and…leather. She felt dizzy. She opened her eyes again and quickly scrabbled to push the buttons through the holes to close the shirt.

Her nipples scraped almost painfully against the lace of her bra. She drew the line at taking that off even though it too was damp.

She'd assumed—since no one had lit her sexual fire before now—that she was somehow not that interested in sex. It turned out she just hadn't met the right man. How galling to find this out in the presence of the man she'd decided wasn't appropriate husband material.

She picked up her ruined shirt and turned around to face the man, fully intending to tell him that she didn't need any further help, but he was already crossing the room and taking the shirt out of her hand and his bare chest was distracting her all over again.

He went to the door and handed her shirt over to some unseen person, giving instructions. He closed the door and faced her. His shirt felt voluminous on Poppy.

He put out a hand, for all the world as if this were his

home and she were his guest. 'Please, make yourself comfortable. They're going to either wash and dry the shirt, or try to source one in the same size. You'll be back in the ballroom before you know it. I've asked for some refreshments. I don't know about you but those canapés weren't making up for my lack of dinner.'

Against her will, Poppy found herself gravitating closer to him and taking a seat. As if he had some sort of hypnotic power over her. But then, she reasoned with herself, when else was she going to get a chance to have an anonymous one-on-one moment with Caius?

The fact that he was an inveterate charmer was confirmed beyond any doubt. He smiled at her now as he also took a seat in a chair opposite her and she was glad she was sitting down.

Ingrained manners forced her to say, 'Thank you for your assistance.'

He shook his head. 'The least I could do when it was entirely my fault. And anyway, the crowd were boring me. I didn't see you arrive. I would have noticed you, dressed so uniquely.'

The confirmation that her new-found confidence and style *had* made an impact was eclipsed by the fact that Caius's bare chest was seriously distracting. She wanted to ask him to put on his jacket. But she didn't want to draw attention to the fact that she found him attractive. And lounging in his open jacket with no shirt on could be even more disturbing. As it was, with his *Zorro*-style mask, he looked utterly roguish.

He leant forward with a hand out. 'I'm—'

'I'd really prefer if we didn't exchange names,'

Poppy blurted out. Her face got warm under his narrowed gaze. He must suspect she knew exactly who he was but if they didn't exchange names then she could somehow pretend that what she was doing here was sanctioned.

He pulled his hand back and regarded her for a long moment. 'OK, no names.' He was clearly intrigued.

Poppy cursed herself. She didn't want to intrigue him. She'd seen enough of the man to know that everything that had been said about him was true. *And the part about him being so solicitous and attentive?* The contradiction stuck under her skin like a burr. She wasn't being entirely fair. He made her uncomfortable. And she should let him know who she was.

She opened her mouth to put an end to this subterfuge when there was a knock on the door, signalling that someone was back with her shirt? Or a new one? To Poppy's shame, her first reaction wasn't relief, it was something more complicated.

Caius went to the door, unashamedly naked from the waist up, and opened it, admitting a staff member from the hotel. He looked like a manager. Poppy stood up. The man came in with other staff who were carrying trays and she also saw an ice bucket with a bottle of sparkling wine.

She watched as they set out an array of small bites and glasses of water and tall flutes. The man bowed to Caius and Poppy and said to her, 'Madam, we will have your shirt returned as soon as possible, in the meantime please enjoy our hospitality.'

To Poppy's mortification, her belly rumbled a little.

She hadn't eaten much that day and the sight of the delicious bites was too tempting. The staff left the room and Caius sat down again, handing her a plate. She dithered for a moment, knowing she should put an end to this, but, instead of putting an end to it, she took the plate and sat back down, asking herself what harm if she had something to eat first? She put some food on her plate and saw Caius loading up his own plate. He obviously had a healthy appetite. He glanced at her and commented, 'You didn't eat much today either?'

She shook her head, feeling guilty. 'No, meetings all day before I came to the party.' She had no need to feel guilty, she had actually met some French trade ministers to discuss business.

'Me too,' he said, then he put a hand to his mask and said, 'Do you mind?'

'No,' she said faintly and watched as he took it off, revealing his face in full. She felt another jolt of electricity. He truly was astoundingly good-looking. Feeling a bit stiff, she said, 'I hope you don't mind if I don't...remove my mask.' She'd already removed her shirt. Her mask felt like a necessary barrier to...this onslaught on her senses she hadn't expected.

'Not at all, whatever makes you comfortable.' He put some food in his mouth, utterly at ease, even half naked, with a total stranger.

She wondered if he really had been in meetings all day, but then Poppy supposed it was a bit unfair to imagine that he'd been lolling around in a bed with a lover. After all, he had taken enough time out of partying to make his own fortune and to be crowned king.

It struck her then that she was rarely in a room with someone who was going through similar challenges to her and that she could even ask him about what it was like to go from crown prince to king, but then she'd have to reveal her own identity and she didn't want to know what kind of look he'd have on his face if he knew she was *her*. The woman who wasn't his type.

She tried to eat and not be distracted by his bare torso or the fact that even sitting down there wasn't a roll of excess flesh. He was as tight as a drum. He opened the wine and held up her glass in question. Something reckless moved through Poppy. 'Yes, please.'

'What do you do?' he asked as he poured wine and handed her the glass, and Poppy had to remember what he was asking her.

She said, 'Um, I'm in the civil service.' Just at a very senior level. She took a generous sip of wine. 'What do you do?' she asked, curious as to how he'd respond.

He swallowed his food and smiled at her. 'Similar, and I'm also in finance.'

She couldn't help smiling. There was something a little exhilarating about being in the lion's den like this. Playing this game.

Another knock on the door and the staff reappeared to take away their food and a young man arrived with Poppy's shirt, impeccably washed and dried and ironed, on a hanger. Instantly she felt a sense of deflation. Their time was over.

CHAPTER TWO

Caius watched as the woman stood and took her shirt from the hotel staff member. He couldn't recall a time when he'd met someone so…reticent. Reluctant to make themselves known to him. She had to know who he was. He wasn't being arrogant, it was just a statement of fact.

Since he'd been crowned king, the press had been even more voracious in their appetite for following him. But this woman didn't seem remotely interested or impressed.

She could be playing a game. Feigning disinterest. It had happened before. Women trying to get Caius's attention by any means. But this time, he hated to admit it, if it was her agenda, it was working. Because he was intrigued. Even more so when his shirt had never looked so sexy on him as it did on her.

Did she realise that she'd buttoned it up haphazardly so he could see tantalising glimpses of her lace-clad breasts through the gaps between the buttonholes?

And she didn't want names exchanged. He found that somewhat refreshing. Even though he felt almost certain she knew who he was, it was nice to not feel the weight of his title or name or history for a moment.

The staff member walked out and Caius stood too and she looked at him. Her dark hair was coming loose from its knot and he had an urge to undo it completely and spear it with his hands, tilting her face up so he could cover her mouth with his and see if she tasted as tempting as she looked.

The mask was lace and seemed to enhance her features. Drawing the eye to those magnificent cheekbones. Her eyes were dark, long lashes.

She put her hand to his shirt and said, 'I guess I should return this.'

The air between them was suddenly charged. Caius glanced at the door. There was a lock. His blood started to sizzle. This was so unexpected…so illicit. And yet a moment of weariness caught at him to recognise that if he was to pursue this feeling of electricity in the air, if he was to try and seduce this woman, this stranger, he would be living up to the reputation that had settled like concrete around him. People would expect nothing less of the playboy prince.

But right now all he could see when he looked back was *her*. Looking at him from under that mask. All at once provocative, and so alluring. And he knew that once he chose a queen, moments like this would be few and far between because he would have to conduct his private liaisons with military-level discretion. He wasn't going to follow in his parents' footsteps and conduct marital affairs to inflict maximum pain on his spouse.

But right now he didn't have a queen. He had this moment to seize.

Caius said with a smile, 'I could leave you in my shirt and wear yours but somehow I don't think I'd look as good in your shirt as you look in mine.'

Colour turned her cheeks pink. She was blushing? Definitely not a reaction Caius was used to.

Then she said, 'Are you saying you like what you see?'

The air got thicker. Caius's cock thickened and grew hard. *Deus.* He wanted her. He nodded, looking down over her body, taking his time. Almost insolent. Leaving her in no doubt what he meant when he said, 'Yes, very much.'

King Caius Mansur de Roche, the man who had declared that she wasn't his type, wanted her. She could see it in his eyes. They were even more piercing. She couldn't help her gaze dropping and her pulse sped up when she saw the unmistakable bulge pressing against his trousers.

He was hard for her. Her heart pounded and her skin felt tight. Poppy was so tempted right now to behave more audaciously than she'd ever behaved. For once her security weren't breathing down her neck; they'd been instructed to stay in the lobby of the hotel. So she was alone in a room with the sexiest man she'd ever met and he wanted her.

The advantage that she had in knowing who he was meant that she also knew that this kind of liaison was common for him. It would mean nothing.

She wouldn't ever marry this man but she could know him in the most intimate way. She could do this and walk away and he would never even know who he'd had sex with. As if he'd even remember her anyway, among the hordes of his other lovers.

Sex. Her heart pounded. Was she really contemplating this? Giving her innocence away before marriage? Oh, she was under no romantic illusions. The chances of her marrying for love—even if that did exist—were slim to none.

Not that she ever aspired to being in love. The thought of being vulnerable enough to lower her emotional guard and allow a man to hurt her was anathema. But so was the thought of still being a virgin on her wedding night. She wasn't some medieval princess. She was a modern woman and she would have slept with someone by now if the oportunity had afforded itself.

It hadn't. Until now. There was also something deliciously ironic about giving her innocence to a king. To the king who had essentially called her boring.

Before she lost her nerve Poppy said, 'Are you saying you want me?'

A muscle in his jaw bulged. 'Do I really need to spell it out?'

He wasn't used to answering questions. She got that. Someone in his position rarely had to justify or clarify. But she needed to be clear. She had no intention of being made a fool of, or exposing herself.

Displaying a confidence she really wasn't feeling, Poppy said, 'Tell them we don't want to be disturbed and lock the door.'

His eyes flared and her pulse thundered. She wondered if she'd stepped over a line. But he was walking towards the door now, every movement fluid with animalistic grace. Confident. He opened the door, issued a command she didn't hear and then closed the door and locked it.

He turned around and rested back against the door for a moment. 'Now you have me here all to yourself.'

Poppy suddenly felt nervous, on the verge of giggling at the audacity of her actions and also deadly serious. 'Come here,' she said, feeling a creeping vulnerability. *No.* There was no need for vulnerability. She was just taking something for herself. Something she could bring with her as she stepped into her future. A secret she would never share.

Caius came back towards her. Bare chest gleaming in the low lights. He stopped a foot away. She looked up at him. His eyes were very blue. He said, 'Take off my shirt.'

For a second as she looked at his bare chest taking up most of her vision Poppy didn't understand what he meant and then it clicked. His shirt, *on her.* Oh.

She looked down and realised that the shirt was gaping a little because she'd done the buttons up wrong. She slipped them through the holes until they were all undone and the shirt fell open but not all the way. Hanging off the edges of her breasts.

'May I?'

She looked up at Caius. She wasn't sure what he was asking but she nodded. He stepped forward, closing the distance between them. And then he put his hands out and pulled apart the shirt.

Poppy heard his indrawn breath and saw the way his

eyes widened. She felt a surge of very feminine pride. She knew she wasn't anything spectacular but under his gaze she felt as though she might be something a little more than average.

He breathed out, 'You are stunning.'

Poppy felt her cheeks heat. She knew she was more womanly than the fashionably stylish ideal. She'd never fitted into sample sizes and working with Clotilde was the first time she'd had a stylist who got who she really was. Even down to her underwear, forcing Poppy to throw out the far more serviceable items she was used to wearing.

So Caius was looking at the new adventurous Poppy. Whose breasts were encased in sheer silk and lace.

Caius gently pushed the shirt off her shoulders and it fell down, all the way to the floor. He put his hands on her bare waist and the feel of his warm palms touching her sent a shock wave through her body. She put her hands on his arms to steady herself. He was warm, muscles taut.

His gaze moved up to her face. Poppy bit her lip, her eyes fixed on his mouth. The strong sensual contours. Giving into an impulse too strong to ignore, she reached up and touched his mouth with her index finger. Tracing its shape. Caius opened his mouth and nipped at her finger, stroking it with his tongue. It was shockingly intimate and yet Poppy couldn't pull away. She was mesmerised by the sensations moving through her body. Electricity. Liquid heat…a pulse between her legs.

She was swaying towards Caius and he tugged her

closer, until her breasts were pressed against his chest and abdomen. He caught her wrist and brought her hand down from his mouth. Then he speared his other hand into her hair and undid it, letting it fall around her shoulders. 'You have beautiful hair,' he said thickly. Poppy felt her conscience twinge. Not her natural hair colour. Maybe if he saw that he'd recognise who he was with and be turned off?

Wanting to distract him, she said, 'Kiss me?'

He looked down at her. His eyes were darker blue now. Like hard sapphires. It made Poppy shiver a little. Wondering what it would take to make this man lose his composure, and suddenly wanting to be the one to do that.

His head was lowering now, slowly, as if giving her time to be sure of what she wanted. Poppy hadn't expected him to be so…considerate. When his mouth touched hers it was warm and firm, she opened a little on a sigh and any sense of consideration was gone.

Breaths mingling, Caius kissed her harder and Poppy's blood leapt and her hands clutched at whatever she could find. Caius's bulging muscles. She opened to him, instinctively, like a flower blooming under the rays of the sun. The kiss went deeper, tongues touching and dancing, stoking flames within Poppy that she'd never felt before.

She felt a delicious tightening sensation deep in her belly, a tension that Caius stoked with his masterful touch. He moved his free hand to her back, pressing her closer. She could feel the thrust of his erection against her belly. His hand moved up her back to the opening of her bra, toying with it.

He pulled back from the kiss and Poppy felt dizzy. She looked up at him, the rush of blood and desire pounding like waves through her body.

He asked, 'Do you mind?'

She shook her head and he snapped open her bra and then pulled back a little to pull it away from her body. He looked at her, at her bare breasts. She felt her nipples puckering, hard.

He reached out and cupped her, feeling the weight of her flesh in his hands. They weren't soft hands. They were hard. Like a working man's. Poppy shoved that titbit aside. It was hard to focus when his thumbs were now teasing her nipples, making them harder.

And then he stopped for a second. 'You have a birthmark.'

Poppy nodded. She did, a little heart-shaped strawberry birthmark under her breast. She tensed, thinking that maybe this would put him off, but he touched her there, moved his thumb over and back, like a kind of benediction. For someone who had never felt enough, the gesture made her feel a spike of emotion.

Caius looked at her. 'You are…a fantasy I never knew I had.'

The emotion swelled. Her legs almost buckled at the reverence in his voice. As if sensing her weakness he tugged her with him as he sat on the couch behind her and she came down with him, landing into his lap.

He held her easily, arms strong around her. She wanted to taste him again so she pressed her mouth against his and he met her, stroke for stroke, finding her breast and squeezing the plump, firm flesh. He broke the kiss so that he could kiss his way across her jaw, down her neck and lower, to her breast where he found one hard, tingling peak and sucked it into his mouth, hot tongue swirling and teeth nipping.

Poppy was clutching Caius, helpless against the waves of pleasure that undulated through her body from her core. As if sensing her need for more, Caius pulled his mouth away and looked at her. His hair was messy. Had she done that?

He put her away from him for a moment and then he stood up. Poppy was splayed on the couch. Naked from the waist up. Caius said, 'I want to see you. All of you.'

'You first,' Poppy said.

He smiled and it was wicked and sexy as he put his hands to his trousers and undid them, opening them and then pulling them down, along with his underwear.

Poppy's eyes widened in silent and very feminine appreciation as she took in his unashamedly virile response. He was…big. And flatteringly hard. His thighs were thickly muscled. Hips narrow.

'Now you.'

Poppy stood up on shaky legs. She undid her trousers and pulled them down but left on her underwear. Caius looked her over. Poppy had never been so studied She was in her head so much that it was liberating to be so aware of her body for once. She felt very primal in that moment, forgetting who Caius was. He was a man and she was a woman and they wanted each other.

'Lie down on the couch,' Caius said.

Poppy obeyed. Lying back into the cushions and watching as Caius grabbed something from his trouser pocket. Protection. He put it to one side. Not even that reminder of his profligacy could take her out of this heady moment. The clamour of her body to be joined with his.

He came down on his knees by the couch and put his hands on her legs, smoothing them up all the way to her underwear, hooking his fingers into the sides and then pulling it down. Poppy felt a moment of panic when she realised that her hair colour wouldn't match the hair between her legs but the light was dim in the room and maybe Caius wouldn't notice too much…

She held her breath as he exposed her to his gaze, throwing her underwear to one side. He pushed her legs apart. Poppy had never been so exposed before a man. Before anyone. He didn't seem to notice anything awry and Poppy soon forgot about being worried about small details like matching hair colour as he came down between her legs and pressed his mouth to her inner thighs, working his way up to the juncture between her legs where every nerve-ending in her body seemed to be throbbing with need.

Her whole body seized as his tongue touched the folds of her sex. It was so intimate, so shocking and like nothing she'd ever experienced. With the flat of his tongue he licked his way into her, spreading her for him and then he explored deeper, and then with his fingers…he breathed against her skin, 'You're so ready for me…'

Poppy was teetering on the brink of something she

desperately needed. An orgasm. She'd tried to pleasure herself before now but had always been interrupted or too tense to fully let go, but now she was liquid heat and with one more flick of Caius's tongue against her, she fell over the edge into an endless clasping wave of pleasure. Gasping for air, hands in Caius's hair. Back arched.

When she floated back down to earth he was rolling a protective sheath onto his aroused body. She gave thanks that he had safety in mind because her mind was blank of everything. She'd taken the pill as an optimistic precaution in university but since her return to Valdere, she'd stopped, feeling a bit ridiculous because the likelihood of sleeping with anyone before a wedding was going to be even less.

She hadn't counted on this moment.

He came over her, on his hands, protecting her from his weight, but she reached for him, wanting his weight on her. In her. They moved together as though they'd done this a million times before. Poppy was the most pragmatic person she knew but right now she almost believed in fate and things like eternal mates because this felt so...*right.*

Caius issued a little curse. 'I don't want to hurt you. I'm big and you're tight.'

Poppy urged him on. 'You won't.' She'd always been active. She knew what to expect losing her virginity but she really didn't think—a long low moan escaped her lips as Caius gave into her entreaty and entered her, breaching her body with his thick girth, pushing deeper.

Poppy's body adjusted quickly, and she lifted her

hips a little, making him go even deeper. They both breathed out. Poppy noticed their skin was slick. Caius took one of her hands and interlaced their fingers, bringing it up above her head. He kissed her as he drove into her, before pulling back out, and then in again, sparking a million and one pleasure zones throughout her body.

She gripped his hip with her other hand, fingers digging into his skin, as their movements became faster, and more urgent.

'*Deus*, I can't…hold on much longer…'

Poppy's sentiments exactly. Her body was primed and ready to explode into pieces all over again and with Caius's next thrust into her body, Poppy splintered around him, her body milking his and sending him over his own edge as he tensed and his hips jerked against hers.

Their hands were clasped so tightly she knew he'd have the marks of her nails on his skin. The thought of that, marking him in some way, was deeply satisfying. She shuddered against him as aftershocks of pleasure made her muscles contract around him and he came down over her, breathing harshly.

They stayed like that for a long moment and then Caius extricated himself from her embrace and manoeuvred them so that he lay on his back and bore her weight.

She was limp with exhaustion but also a burgeoning sense of wonder and exhilaration. *So that was sex.* Good sex. Amazing sex. Feeling the way she did right now, floating on a cloud of sated bliss, Poppy could almost forgive Caius his lifestyle. If sex was this good… she could become addicted herself.

For a few seconds, she dozed off, cheek resting against Caius's chest, arm across his torso. His arm around her. But then she jerked awake again when there was a sound from outside the room.

She looked at Caius. He was asleep. Lashes long and dark on his cheek. Ridiculously long lashes. They should have made him look pretty but they only made him look even more masculine. He also looked more serious in sleep. Less…frivolous.

Realising she was welded to him and staring at him like some kind of lovestruck groupie, Poppy started to extricate herself as slowly as she could so as not to disturb him. When she'd freed herself and stood up, she realised her legs were like jelly.

Caius made a sound and moved slightly but didn't open his eyes. Poppy froze. She guiltily took a last look at his impressive body—even at rest—before she gathered up her things, and her freshly cleaned shirt, and got dressed.

She had to leave now. She'd danced with the devil and she didn't want him waking and finding her still here. This had been a dangerously illicit moment. Indulgent. Crazy.

Poppy had pulled on her clothes haphazardly, her fresh shirt, slipped her feet back into her shoes, and had a hand on the door lock when she heard a rustling sound from behind her and froze.

'Hey, where are you going?'

His voice was rough and it sent fresh sparks of

awareness into Poppy's blood. Reluctantly she turned around. Caius was up on one elbow on the couch, long powerful body on its side.

She swallowed. 'I have to go.'

'Do you?'

'Yes.'

'I don't even know your name.'

'I'm no one special, really.' An old wound reactivated. If she'd been a boy she'd have been deemed more special by her father. *But Caius had just made her feel special.*

He sat up now and Poppy moved back against the door. If he came close to her again there was no telling what she'd do. She'd just behaved more uncharacteristically than she'd ever done in her life.

But he stayed on the couch and said, 'I want to see you again.'

Something inside her leapt at that but then deflated again when she realised that he thought he was saying this to a complete stranger. But she knew he was in talks with *her* to become her husband. And, if not her, then someone else very soon.

Poppy seized on this to make her move. Caius was showing her his true colours. And it was nothing she didn't already know. He'd told her how he would envision a marriage—conducting separate lives except for coming together to have children, and continuing his liaisons outside that. That was not the father material she wanted for her children.

She wanted someone who would be by her side—she wanted to succeed where her father had failed. She wasn't asking for a love match; she was happy to keep some emotional distance, but she wanted loyalty and fidelity. A better father for her children than she'd had.

And after what she'd just experienced, she knew that repeating *that* for the sake of procreating and nothing more was far too disturbing to her to investigate and that terrified her.

She shook her head. 'Sorry, but I have to go.'

She turned the lock on the door and opened it and slipped out. Caius's security was standing outside and she didn't make eye contact. She figured that he had seen this scenario a hundred times before.

A couple of days later, Poppy had Stephen send word to King Caius's people that she was no longer interested in pursuing discussions about a royal union. Stephen remonstrated with her but Poppy remained adamant. The fact that it had more to do with her reaction to him personally and physically than her lofty dreams to have an engaged partner and committed loving father for her children was a shameful secret she would never reveal.

Then, a couple of days after that, Stephen came into her office and put down the daily papers, saying grimly, 'Looks like your instincts were right all along.'

The papers were full of King Caius's latest scandal. It had been discovered that he wasn't in fact the biological son of the late king of Sadat Sur Mer. He was the product of an affair his mother, the late queen, had had.

King Caius announced his abdication not long afterwards. His younger sister would now be crowned as queen. Poppy felt a measure of sympathy for the young woman.

Poppy would never admit it, but instead of relief that the question of Caius's suitability had now been shut down completely, what she did feel was infinitely more disturbing to name.

CHAPTER THREE

Wedding Day

'I'M NO ONE SPECIAL.' Caius looked out of the small aeroplane window taking in the view of the verdant mountainous region below, with its picturesque main city spread along the shores of a sparkling lake.

He couldn't deny that Valdere was a stunningly beautiful country. *Like its crown princess.* His jaw got tight. The woman who had exposed his attraction to her, while keeping her identity a secret, before walking away and saying those words, *I'm no one special.* How she must have laughed at his cluelessness. At the way he'd begged her for more. To see her again. For her name.

She had been special enough to haunt his every waking moment and dreams, even as his life had imploded around him upon the revelations that he was not his father's son. That he was not in fact the rightful heir to the throne of Sadat Sur Mer.

And it hadn't just been because she'd been the first woman to walk away from him. She'd been the first woman to ignite his libido in a way that had felled him with its force.

He'd actually begun to doubt that night had even happened, wondered if he'd conjured her up, until she'd appeared in his offices in Manhattan a month ago and had dropped the bombshell that she was far from *no one special.* She was in fact a crown princess and she was pregnant with his child.

The same crown princess who he'd been in talks with to consider marriage. The same crown princess who in the days after that night in Paris had sent a message telling him she wasn't going to pursue discussions of a marriage.

This was *after* sleeping with him. And *before* he'd lost his crown. When he'd still been one of the most sought-after bachelors in the world.

The fact that she'd only then sought him out because she was pregnant had added salt to the wound of his sense of exposure and humiliation. Something he would never reveal.

Nor would he ever reveal that just before she'd reappeared in his life, when he'd been coming out of the other end of those tumultuous months, he'd been feeling rudderless and untethered, not sure how to navigate his new existence as a disgraced ex-king.

Not even the fact that he now had a reason for why his father had always looked at him with some level of suspicion had helped all that much. Or that it had gone some way to explaining the very toxic nature of his parents' fraught marriage.

No, all he could see in his mind's eye was *her*, in his office, in slim-fitting dark trousers, with a silk shirt buttoned up to her neck with a provocative pussy-bow tie, hair sleek and pulled back, looking every inch the European princess. Looking nothing like the woman he'd slept with in Paris. Because this woman had red hair. Not brown. And green eyes. Not dark.

But before he'd recognised who she really was, and before her bombshell announcement, Caius had been confused as to why she'd wanted to see him. After all, she'd called a halt to marriage negotiations before he'd had to abdicate.

'Why are you here, Princess Poppy? You made it pretty clear we had little to discuss even before I had to abdicate. Unless you're here on other business? Looking for financial advice?'

She'd blurted out, 'Did you know?'

Caius had known instantly her meaning and his insides had clenched hard. 'Did I know what? That I was a bastard?'

She'd winced but he'd felt no remorse.

'I don't think that word is really necessary,' she'd said primly.

He'd raised a brow. 'It's the word people are attaching to me, with not a little relish. Everyone enjoys a spectacular downfall.'

She'd gestured around her at Caius's penthouse office. 'You're not doing too badly considering.'

'No,' he'd agreed, 'I'm not. Because contrary to popular opinion I haven't actually spent the last decade falling out of a nightclub, I've been growing a financial business. And, not that it's any of your business, but no, I had no idea I wasn't the king's son. It was as much of a shock to me as everyone else.'

To his surprise she'd said huskily, 'I can only imagine how unsettling that must have been. And for your sister, too.' Something about the tone of her voice had caught in his gut. As if he'd heard her speak before. Saying something else. Something altogether more… provocative. He'd been afraid he was losing it. And he'd had no time for rubber-necking princesses who wanted to see the disgraced ex-king up close.

He'd looked at his watch, 'Look, I have a meeting to get to.'

'No, you don't. I looked at your assistant's agenda while she was in here.'

Caius's hackles had gone up. He wasn't used to anyone questioning him. 'I don't have to justify my schedule to anyone and we have nothing more to discuss.'

But she hadn't moved. She'd said, 'We do have something to discuss. Something rather…big. Related to that night in Paris.'

Caius had frowned. 'Paris? That night? What night?'

'The night we met…at the party. Not long before your, er, abdication was announced.'

Caius's eyes had narrowed on her. What the *hell*? 'I was only at one party in Paris in the last few months. You definitely were not there.'

Poppy had looked pale. 'Oh, I can assure you I was there, and that we met.'

'We did not.'

'Yes,' Poppy had reiterated firmly. 'I was wearing a tuxedo suit and we became…quite well acquainted, after you spilled your drink on me and caused me to spill mine too. I had to replace my shirt.'

Caius had gone hot and then cold. 'How do you even know about that?'

'Because I was there. That was me.'

His voice had felt constricted. 'Impossible.'

'Oh no, it's quite possible, believe me.'

Caius had felt as if he'd moved through some invisible portal to a place where people said nonsensical things. Princesses, specifically. He'd shaken his head as if that might help things come back to normal.

But no, the princess had still been standing in his office looking at him. A total *stranger*. Except she'd been saying she wasn't. That, in fact, they'd been intimate.

The thought that it had been her was too huge to try and accept. He'd gone into full denial mode. 'No, you're somehow privy to this information and now you're out to extort something from me.'

She'd muttered something as she'd laid her bag down at her feet and stood up again. Then he'd watched as she'd untucked her shirt from her trousers and started to unbutton it from the bottom. Caius's eyes had widened and awareness had leapt in his blood as he'd watched creamy skin being revealed, the curve of her waist. Flashes of memory had come back. Her wearing his shirt.

And then, as if in slow motion, she'd been exposing the full underside of her breast, encased in lace and silk. He'd moved forward without even making the conscious decision. So he could better see the distinctive mark under her breast. A small heart-shaped strawberry birthmark.

He'd recalled touching it. *You have a birthmark.*

Caius had dragged his gaze back up to her face, recognising those lines. The even features. The slight dimple in her chin. But…

'Your hair was dark…and your eyes were not green.'

She'd had the grace to look discomfited as she'd rebuttoned her shirt and tucked it back into her trousers. 'I dyed my hair with a wash-out colour and put contact lenses in.'

Caius had taken a step back, suddenly needing distance between them. 'Why?'

Her cheeks had been pink. 'I wanted to see what you were like…in person. I wasn't sure about the engagement.'

'And you couldn't just come up to me, tap me on the shoulder and introduce yourself like a regular person?'

She'd flushed even more and that had only made Caius think of how she'd looked as she'd lain back on the couch in that room and had offered herself up to him. And the way he'd fallen on her like a drowning man. More turned on than he had been in a long time. *Since then.*

She'd lifted her chin. 'Let's just say I didn't feel confident of the reception I'd receive considering how I wasn't…' she used air quotes '…your *type*.'

The fact that she most certainly had been his type had made him burn inside. 'What are you talking about?'

She'd looked uncomfortable. 'My chief counsellor and I overheard your conversation with your people before we spoke on the phone. You didn't realise that we'd connected in…'

Caius had cast his mind back and recalled talking about her, admitting that she wasn't his type and that all he'd need from her would be heirs and then she could get on with her life and he could get on with his.

He'd had the grace to admit stiffly, 'It wasn't meant for your ears.'

Princess Poppy had shrugged minutely. 'It was unfortunate timing. But that's why I wanted to go incognito, so I could see what you were like in…person. To see if we could be compatible in spite of the way you'd dismissed me.'

A flash of heat had gone straight to Caius's cock when he'd thought of how compatible they'd been, making it twitch. 'I think we proved that point.'

Caius's cock was twitching again now, just at that memory. He shifted in the plane seat as they started to descend to land at the small Valdere airport. The fact that, in spite of everything, she could still have this effect on him was deeply disturbing and unwelcome.

Especially when he now knew the real reason she'd sought him out. Because that night they'd conceived. The moment she'd told him was as brutally vivid as the other memories.

But before she'd told him, he'd found himself watching her as she'd looked around his office and out at the view. Her lustrous red hair, and that creamy complexion. Huge green eyes, like emeralds. How had he ever dismissed her as not his type? She was absolutely stunning.

Something else had replaced the shock of learning her real identity. A spurt of adrenalin. Excitement.

Caius had had no reason not to deduce that if she had come to him then clearly she still wanted something. *Him.* Maybe she'd realised she'd been too quick to walk away. Maybe she wanted to continue what they'd shared that night.

Feeling as if he was on firmer ground since the moment she'd walked into his office—for the first time in weeks—Caius had sat back in his chair and when she'd looked back at him, he'd smiled at her and noticed how her eyes had flared and widened. A response that had merely confirmed his suspicions.

'I'm pleased that you came.'

She'd swallowed visibly. 'You are?'

He'd nodded, and smiled wider, a smile that had never failed him before. 'Yes, because I haven't been able to get you out of my head. Clearly we still want each other, and I see no reason why we can't pick up where we left off.'

And at that moment the plane landed in Valdere with a jolt and but not even that could pull Caius from the past, because, contrary to his arrogant assumption that Poppy had wanted to see him again, *that* was when she'd dropped the bombshell, saying, 'I came here today not because I wanted to see you again but to tell you I'm twelve weeks pregnant. With your baby.'

For a long moment the words had hung in the air between them. Benign. And then, Caius had said hoarsely, 'We used protection. *I* used protection.'

'Evidently it failed.'

'Not possible.'

'Statistically, yes, it is possible. Can you be certain it didn't fail?'

Caius had felt that sting of exposure again to acknowledge that he'd been so hot for her that he obviously hadn't paid as much attention as he might have usually.

'Your Highness?'

Caius looked up at the air steward. He realised he was scowling and rearranged his expression. 'Yes?'

The steward cleared his throat. 'Um, we're here, in Valdere. If you want any help changing into your wedding suit, please just call me.'

Caius had arranged to have the wedding suit brought on the plane. He'd planned on changing before landing but the memories had haunted him the whole way across the Atlantic ocean.

He emitted a curse and undid his seat-belt buckle, standing up and heading for the bedroom where the suit was laid out. He could see SUVs waiting outside. Sleek. With the flags of both Sadat Sur Mer and Valdere fluttering in the warm breeze. They might as well be prison vans.

The fact that in spite of everything he was somehow still destined to be a king was ironic in the extreme. Of course, he'd challenged Poppy on the assumption that he was the father.

'How do you know it's even mine? You weren't shy that night, you must have had other lovers.'

'For your information,' she'd gritted out, two spots of red high in each cheek, 'you were my first and only lover.'

Caius had looked at her. And then he'd let out a bark of laughter in sheer disbelief.

She'd looked insulted. 'What is so funny about that?'

He'd stopped laughing long enough to say, 'Because virgins are about as mythical as unicorns. How old are you? Twenty-five? Where have you been? Under a rock? You're a beautiful woman, it's impossible you were still an innocent.'

To Caius's surprise, he'd seen something like hurt cross Poppy's face before she'd stood up and was almost at the door of his office before she'd stopped and turned around. 'I didn't come here to be ridiculed.'

Caius had been so shocked to see a woman walk away from him—*for the second time*—that it had taken him a moment to realise what was happening and go after her. He'd taken her to his apartment because even if she had been lying about the baby, about her innocence, it was clear he had to know what her agenda was because he *had* slept with her.

As for whether or not he was the father, he'd had to concede uncomfortably that he did believe her because Poppy and her people had shut down engagement talks *before* he'd had to abdicate. So if she was just looking for a convenient baby daddy, he wasn't going to be top of the list, which made it more believable that he *was* likely to be the father.

When Caius had realised that, he'd waited for a sense of panic to hit. A sense of rejection. But it hadn't come. What he had felt was something more ambiguous. He'd always known he'd have to have children but he'd seen it as a necessary duty and he'd vowed to himself he would do his best not to put them through the same emotional trauma his parents had inflicted on him and his sister.

Caius had been pretty confident that, with choosing the right woman to be his queen and with the best staff money could buy, his children couldn't possibly fare any worse. But Caius was no longer a king. He no longer had to play by those rules. He'd said, 'If the child is mine, and of course that will have to be proved with a DNA test when it's born, how do you want to proceed? We can come to some arrangement.'

Against the backdrop of his Manhattan apartment Poppy had looked at him and her eyes had widened. '*The child?* You mean your son, or daughter.'

Caius hadn't liked the little jolt he'd felt in his gut to think of that. 'I am aware it could be a child of either sex.'

'You are going to be involved with your son or daughter, in a meaningful way. Not just as a financial support.'

'What are you saying exactly?' But even as he'd asked that he'd already known what she would say. Because it was the only option for people like them. He was still considered royalty even if his blood was more diluted than previously believed. He'd been born into privilege and the knowledge that one day he would rule.

The fact that he could be free of that heavy burden of duty was a concept he'd still been getting his head around. The fact that he wouldn't have to be responsible for bringing a child into this world for one reason only—to be of service and continue a bloodline—had been liberating.

Except that had no longer been the case.

So when Poppy had said, 'Well, that we will be married, of course,' Caius hadn't so much as flinched. Because he and Princess Poppy of The House of Valdun were not normal people. They came from a world where their actions were held up to the public and scrutinised and discussed. They came from immense privilege and wealth and this was their due. To be held accountable for moments of weakness.

His newfound sense of freedom had already been dead in the water.

And then he'd remembered something and pointed at her. 'You did this on purpose, because you can't become queen until you marry.'

She'd gone pale, but two spots of colour had been high in her cheeks. 'I did not set out that night to sleep with you, or conceive. Believe it or not, I have a little more integrity than that. I would never choose deception as a means to bring a child into this world.'

'Yct you hid your idenitity.'

'I already told you why I went incognito.'

Yes, she had. And Caius *had* had that unfortunate conversation in her earshot. He'd also just conveniently forgotten that she'd rejected him *before* he'd had to abdicate.

Something inside him had deflated. She hadn't tried to trap him but she was evidently pregnant. It would be a small matter to confirm the DNA when the child was born but Caius had known the chances of her lying were slim. No one would invite the backlash that such a discovery would bring, and she didn't strike him as the type to invite that kind of notoriety.

And he'd known that, after his own experiences, he could never let any child of his be born and grow up questioning their place in the world, or their identity.

They would know who their father was and where they came from. And that was the only reason he was here today to marry Poppy Valdun. They were to be married for a minimum of five years. She'd wanted for ever. He'd wanted one year. They'd compromised.

He'd figured that five years would give the child a chance to feel settled and secure and then Caius would have no problem cutting ties with the marriage and seeking out his freedom again. He would of course maintain contact with his child—they wouldn't suffer because of his moment of ill judgement.

At least his child would know who their parents were and even though he didn't know Poppy all that well, he somehow sensed instinctively she would be a better mother than his own had been. So, as far as he was concerned, his kid was already winning at life.

As for them, him and Poppy? That one night had had too many consequences to even think about repeating. And they didn't need to. She was already pregnant.

The fact that Caius still wanted her was an inconvenience, but one that he was sure would fade as soon as they spent time together. That was usually the best solution for killing any desire he had for a woman.

He stood at the door of the aeroplane and looked at

the driver standing next to the open door of the nearest SUV down on the tarmac. Time to get married.

'Poppy?'

Poppy turned around to look at Stephen. She'd completely forgotten he was even here, so lost in her thoughts and memories. But reality came crashing back. 'Yes?'

'Prince Caius has landed. He's on the way to the church. We should get moving.'

Poppy's insides clenched. *He'd come.* He'd overcome his resentment and anger for this whole situation and had come to marry her. For the sake of a baby he couldn't stop calling *it*, or, *the child.*

He hadn't been here himself in the run-up to the wedding but his staff had been on hand to help and money had been no object. Poppy supposed she had better get used to the message he was sending loud and clear—he would be available only for the absolute minimum of interaction.

Steeling herself for what lay ahead, Poppy drew herself up straight and said, 'You'd better tell Clotilde and her team to come back in and finish getting me ready.'

As the glam team filed back in and started fussing around her, putting the tiara on her head and attaching the veil, something glinted in the reflection of the mirror and she lifted her hand to look at the antique diamond engagement ring. Caius had had his people send over a selection of rings from the Sadat Sur Mer vaults and she'd chosen this one. Something about it had called to her, in its simplicity. A circular diamond in a square platinum setting with tiny emeralds on each side.

She dropped her hand. So much for a romantic proposal. They couldn't be more removed from that. Poppy put her hand over the still discreet bump. Her belly seemed to be growing daily and she knew that she would do anything for the baby within. Her son or daughter would not know the awful rejection she'd faced just because of her sex.

She would do better and she vowed that Caius would do his bit too. At least with a guarantee of a minimum of five years of marriage, their son or daughter would have both parents in their life for the formative years. She pushed aside the voice that reminded her she'd had both her parents until she was six, not that it had proven all that beneficial in the end.

She tried to ignore the memory of the hurt she'd felt when Caius had made it apparent he wanted to marry for only a year. He'd eventually compromised. He couldn't have made it more clear that he would prefer to be dragged over hot coals than marry her.

As the veil was arranged over her face, obscuring the room around her, Poppy thought to herself that now all she had to do was navigate the next five years living with a man who resented her. Maybe even hated her. Not a problem. She'd done it her whole life with her father. Another few years would be nothing.

'Ready?' It was Stephen's voice.

No, Poppy thought, suddenly dreading seeing Caius's stony expression, but she pushed it down. She couldn't be weak or show any vulnerability. That was why she was here in this situation and that was how you got hurt.

'I'm ready.'

CHAPTER FOUR

CAIUS STOOD AT the altar in his ceremonial wedding suit complete with royal sash and medals. He felt all the eyes on him, avidly watching this prince who'd fallen from grace. Cameras strategically positioned were the portals for God knew how many more around the world.

Of some comfort was his sister, Cassie, in one of the first pews. She'd been crowned Queen of Sadat Sur Mer some weeks ago but familiar guilt and shame rose up within Caius—even though he knew rationally he wasn't to blame for his mother's reckless affair, he couldn't help but feel responsible for the accident of his birth, that he wasn't a full-blooded Mansur. The old wound of feeling as though he had nothing of substance to offer because he'd been born purely to fulfil a role had been compounded by helplessly having to watch Cassie take on a burden she shouldn't have ever had to face.

Caius pushed his introspection aside.

Of course no one believed this union was a real match. And they'd believe it even less when the press annoucement was made about the pregnancy. They'd mutually agreed to do that after the wedding.

The stiff engagement photo that had been taken in Central Park the day after Poppy had dropped her pregnancy bombshell had spoken multitudes. For once Caius had been unable to get over the shock of the pregnancy for long enough to appear charming, his go-to response to pretty much everything.

Even his sister had commented dryly, 'You look like a deer in the headlights. Maybe it's because you're not used to being photographed with women in bright daylight, sober and fully dressed.'

The fact that Caius had still wanted Poppy after exposing himself spectacularly by telling her he wanted to pick up where they'd left off when clearly she'd had no intention of that had contributed to his overall lack of ability to find his usual level of charm.

He gritted his jaw. Not the memory he needed right now as he waited for this farce to begin. He felt as if he'd been standing at the top of the aisle for aeons. Was Princess Poppy going to stand him up? For a moment, his first reaction wasn't one of relief and that irritated him intensely.

Because he truly resented being in this situation. He'd been born to fulfil a role, born to two parents who'd barely tolerated each other. Then he'd been spat out as soon as it had become apparent his blood wasn't pure, only to now be pulled back into that orbit. An orbit that had deemed him unsuitable.

His friend and best man—Ares Drakos, Cassie's fiancé—bent his head towards Caius now and said, 'She's here.'

A little electric tremor went up Caius's spine as the

crowd hushed and the organ started to play. He felt an overwhelming urge to turn but fought it.

They hadn't seen each other since that morning in Central Park and their respective teams had organised everything in the meantime. Maybe when he saw her now he would feel nothing?

But he couldn't deny the sense of anticipation, a prickling under his skin. Fatefully, the fact that no other women had appealed to him since that night in Paris pointed towards her still having an effect on him, and, for a man who'd never expected to actually want his bride beyond doing his royal duty, it was a terrifying prospect.

He scowled at himself. Was he so institutionalised that he'd instinctively sought out a royal mate by sleeping with Poppy that night?

The back of his neck prickled now. He found it was impossible to keep looking away. He slowly turned around to see Poppy moving slowly down the aisle, on her own. He hated the fact that he found her coming to him alone was somehow significant. And made him *feel* something uncomfortable. Empathy. Sympathy.

He sucked in a breath as she came closer. She was encased in white lace, no, not white, a kind of off-white. With a high neck and voluminous satin skirts. The sleeves ended at her elbows.

She wore a sparkling tiara, peeping out from under the veil that obscured her face at the front and trailed behind her at the back.

Her waist looked tiny. He imagined spanning it with his hand. The red of her hair was vibrant enough to be visible under the veil. And as she drew closer, he saw only the faintest indication of her pregnancy, the faintest bulge of her belly under the lace and satin. Bizarrely, Caius felt an urge to reach out and put his hand to her there and curled his hand to a fist to negate it.

Did he imagine it or did he see Poppy's green eyes flicker down to that movement before looking up again?

She held a bouquet of surprisingly humble wild flowers and something about that caught at him. He realised it reminded him of the flowers from Sadat Sur Mer.

And then she was beside him and her distinctive scent mixed with the flowers made him want to breathe deep. She handed her flowers to someone and then went to lift the veil but Caius found himself reaching out so he could do it, pulling up the fine lace to reveal her face, tilted up towards him.

He was so used to seeing women primp and preen and smile for him, but he realised now that, from the moment they'd met, Poppy had always regarded him with a kind of wariness. Had she even smiled that night when they'd combusted? She certainly hadn't flirted. He suddenly wondered what it would be like if she was to smile up at him. Wide and unrestrained. It made his breath catch in his chest.

Her eyes were huge and very green. Mouth full and sheened with the faintest colour. He wanted to skip all of this pomp and crush that mouth under his, slaking his lust and his anger at her for bringing him here, but he knew he couldn't even blame her when *he'd* been the one falling on her like a lust-crazed teen, and then she was saying something and he had to focus.

'Thank you for coming.' Was there the slightest hint of sarcasm? Her voice was low enough for just his ears. Why did that feel intimate when they were in a cathedral surrounded by hundreds of people?

Caius's conscience pricked. He had planned on travelling sooner but he'd been distracted by a financial crisis in the last ten days—but for some reason he didn't say that now. As if it would expose him in some way. 'I'm here for one reason and one reason only—my child.'

'You've made that crystal clear.'

Caius felt off-centre. He usually found it so easy to charm women because he never went any deeper than the most superficial level, but he wasn't charming around Poppy. He was gnarly and prickly. Defensive. But now it was too late to say anything more anyway. The priest was clearing his throat and they had to turn to face him.

Two hours later, Poppy was still reeling. The wedding ceremony had passed in a blur, as had the open-top carriage ride back to the palace through the pretty streets of Valdere thronged with locals and tourists. Whenever she'd snuck glimpses at Caius he'd had a fixed smile on his face as he'd waved. She could at least give thanks he wasn't scowling into the crowds of well-wishers.

And then they'd had the coronation, a swearing-in with her highest-level staff and signing the legal documents decreeing Poppy to be queen, and Caius her king consort. It had always been tradition in the royal house of Valdun to conduct the coronations behind closed doors. Something that had its origins in medieval times when they'd been under threat from neighbouring countries, in case anyone tried to disrupt the process.

And now, they were standing before closed French doors, waiting for them to be opened out onto a balcony. Poppy could hear the crowd outside, people thronging the palace grounds to get their first glimpse of their queen and new king. For a second she felt a spurt of anger at her late father.

If he hadn't made it so hard for her to become queen without a husband she never would have gone to Paris to see Caius up close. She would be here on her own and not with someone by her side who didn't want to be here. She could have chosen her consort at her leisure and picked someone who didn't resent her or make her feel so self-aware.

At that very moment Poppy felt something like a butterfly movement in her abdomen. *The baby.* She put her hand there reflexively and Caius turned his head and looked down. He frowned. 'Are you OK?'

Those were practically the first words he'd spoken to her since the vows they'd exchanged in the cathedral. Poppy nodded, suddenly caught unawares by the rush of emotion she felt at this first tangible evidence of her baby. Apart from the thickening of her waist and the tenderness of her breasts.

She forgot that she'd just been feeling angry to be in this situation with someone who could hardly bring himself to touch her. Their kiss in the cathedral had been a dry peck, so quick that Poppy wasn't even sure it had happened.

But the crowd would expect something more than a peck now. She looked up at Caius beside her. 'You know…the people, they don't know that this isn't a real union.'

He looked at her. 'They're all romantics?'

Poppy could feel her face get warm. 'No, I mean, they're not naive, they'll know it's an arrangement of sorts, but they'll hope that it's real. Even though my father married numerous times they always greeted every new queen like she was the first.'

That had been particularly stinging for Poppy to witness—the way her father had jettisoned her mother and just moved on again, and again and again. She'd given up trying to bond with her new stepmothers when it had become apparent they'd seen her as some kind of a threat. She'd got used to being sidelined. Sent to schools far away.

She'd been sent to America during holidays to spend time with her mother, but her mother hadn't liked to be reminded of the fact that her marriage had failed and, also, she'd been busy trying to keep her successful businessman husband happy, so invariably Poppy had been left to her own devices there too.

Her father had insisted on having main custody only because of a law that decreed the crown heir had to be resident in Valdere. She'd always known as soon as one of her stepmothers had a son, Poppy would most likely have been sent to live with her mother full-time. But none of them had.

She brought her focus back to the present moment. 'It would be good if we can just appear to be united. As much for stability as for the baby's sake. Once the pregnancy news is released and people realise how far along I am, gossip will be inevitable, but hopefully the prospect of a new royal baby will drown it out.'

Caius's eyes were so blue it almost hurt to look at them. Poppy couldn't help but feel he was seeing into her all the way deep down where she longed to know what it felt like to be loved. Really loved. She hated herself for that need, which felt more acute now that she was in a situation with someone who hated her.

'You know what?' she said, looking away. 'Forget I said anything. If you can't even bring yourself to pretend in public that we're united then—'

Caius took her hand and Poppy's words came to an abrupt stop. She looked up at him, her heart suddenly galloping.

He said, 'I agree. I don't want to make this any more challenging than it already will be for our child.'

Poppy had to concede at least that *our child* was an improvement on *the child.* At that moment guards opened the French doors and they walked forward and onto the balcony, hand in hand.

Poppy couldn't help smiling at the sight of the thousands of people and her beautiful country sparkling in the sunshine with the great lake in the distance. Her father's rule hadn't been popular. He'd been so preoccupied with an heir that he'd been a distracted and an increasingly bitter monarch, failing to enjoy what he had under his own nose. A beautiful country and a loyal people.

Even though most of them would know this wasn't a love match, Poppy wanted to provide them with a sense of optimism and hope for a brighter future. They didn't have to know that there was already a time limit on this marriage.

She lifted her hand and waved and Caius waved too. Then it became apparent that the crowd were shouting something, some were saying *'bacio'*, Italian for kiss—one of the main languages in Valdere, nestled as it was between several countries. Some were saying *'bisou'* and most of them were saying *'kiss, kiss'*.

When Poppy looked at Caius he was holding his hand up to his ear as if he couldn't hear them and smiling. Her insides twisted. He could certainly act the part of a besotted newly-wed king. Then he looked at her and Poppy promptly forgot about everyone. All she could see was his mouth. He turned towards her and his free hand was on her jaw and then sliding around to the back of her neck under the low chignon.

He tugged her towards him and Poppy went, and then, as if in slow motion, Caius's head came down, blocking out the sun, and his mouth settled on hers. Warm and firm and…her insides caught fire as memories bombarded her. Of kissing him the first time. Of the way she'd suddenly understood what desire was.

It was happening again except this time with the acute stab of hunger because she knew how good it could be. And she wanted him, with a lustiness that made her feel dizzy. She wasn't prepared for when Caius pulled back, blinking up at him dizzily.

It was only the rapturous clapping and whooping of the crowd and the way Caius straightened up that brought Poppy back down to earth with a thud. She forced a smile back onto her face and waved again before they turned and went back into the formal reception room of the palace.

Aides were waiting. Poppy sought out Stephen's familiar face and he looked at her quizzically as if to ask if she was OK. She nodded her head minutely. But she was not OK. She was a mass of swirling desires and recrimination and very aware of the man just feet away who was being divested of his ceremonial sash and the plumed hat that should have looked ridiculous on him but which had only enhanced his intense masculinity.

At least it wasn't the custom to wear crowns in Valdere. Poppy's head was beginning to ache just from the tiara she wore. The veil had been removed before she'd stepped out onto the balcony.

'The guests await your arrival at the lunch reception, Your Highnesses.' An aide was bowing before them.

They still had a whole formal state lunch banquet to get through before…what? Poppy wasn't even sure what came next. It wasn't as if she'd discussed it with Caius. He was here now, he'd done his duty to make this marriage and pregnancy legitimate.

'Shall we?'

He was beside her, holding out his arm for her to put hers through. Looking about as enthused by this prospect as she was. She might have found that comforting in other circumstances.

'Yes, let's do this.'

As the sun set over the pretty Alpine city, turning the clear sky gold and orange, Caius took a moment and stepped onto an empty balcony off the corridor to breathe some air deep. He was waiting for Poppy to join him so they could enter the ballroom together for the first dance.

What a joke. The whole thing. And yet his conscience pricked. The day had gone off without a hitch. The formal lunch banquet had been refreshingly pleasant—the food unfussy and comprising simple seasonal dishes. There was a laid-back elegance to the proceedings.

It was a surprise because the impression Caius had gleaned of Valdere from his team's research had been that, while it had potential, it was a country stuck culturally in its ways and times, full of the kind of pomp and frills that he hated. Clearly Poppy had brought in fresh air and exactly the changes that Caius would have agreed with.

He saw her now in the corridor outside the main ballroom. His wife. She was being attended to by a stylist who was adjusting her dress and a couple of women were touching up her hair and make-up. She still wore the tiara and he guessed it must hurt after hours of wear. He remembered how his crown had felt on his coronation day—heavy.

His gaze tracked down and, from this side angle, he

could see the faint bulge of her belly. It still confounded him, the thought of a baby.

At that moment, as if aware of his gaze, she looked up and right at him. Finding him without even trying. A strange sense of kinship took Caius by surprise and he remembered feeling it before, when she'd said, *I'm no one special*. And that had been when he hadn't even known just how *un*special he was.

He left the balcony and walked towards her. He said, 'I'm sure you could take the tiara off now, if you want.'

Poppy put her hand up to it and glanced at one of her aides, a younger man Caius had heard her call Stephen. The man shrugged and said, 'No real reason why not—we're at the informal end of things. After the dance you'll be free to leave.'

Poppy looked at one of the women. 'Let's take it off, then. My head is throbbing.'

Caius felt a spurt of something he couldn't initially recognise as he watched the women carefully extract the tiara before tidying up her hair again. He realised it was concern. For her well-being. It had been a long day and she was pregnant. That was all.

She looked at him a little shyly as everyone melted away but for the man Stephen and a couple of other aides who were checking the ballroom. She gave a small smile. 'Thanks for that. It was becoming almost unbearable.'

'I know,' Caius admitted, not liking how her smile made him want to study her mouth. 'I had to wear my crown on my coronation day, for hours. I have to thank you for not making me wear a crown.'

'My father, who was a traditionalist in every other way, had a thing about crowns. He did away with the requirement to wear them.' Something minute crossed her face. 'One of his better ideas.'

Caius found himself wondering about her relationship with the king. He knew she'd been an only child and that there had been the rule that she had to marry to become queen. She'd just said he'd been a tradionalist. He wanted to know more. And he never wanted to know more.

He'd made pretty much a career out of not wanting to know anything too personal about the women he'd been with…telling himself that he was only protecting them from getting any notions that he was interested in a relationship, but, uncomfortably now, he could see that he'd also been protecting himself from getting attached.

Caius wasn't completely delusional, he was well aware that the distinct lack of care in his upbringing had forged a strong desire to deflect everyone from the emptiness he felt inside. The fear that if anyone was to look too closely they'd see that he was really nothing substantial at all.

'Ready, Your Highnesses.'

Caius looked away from Poppy to where a staff member was waiting at the closed doors for their cue. He put out his arm and Poppy slid hers into it. He put his hand over hers, an unconscious gesture.

He looked at her. 'Ready?'

She nodded, looking forward. He said, 'Open the doors.'

The doors swung back and the ballroom was revealed. Impressively majestic with rococo decoration. A parquet floor. Glittering chandeliers. And hundreds of pairs of eyes.

The music from a string quartet struck up as they walked in. A slow waltz. Everyone clapped. The crowd parted and they walked into the empty space in the middle of the room. Caius stood in front of Poppy and lifted her hand and put his arm around her back.

They moved smoothly together, both trained for this from almost as soon as they could walk.

'I have to apologise,' Caius heard himself saying.

Poppy looked up. 'You do?'

He nodded. 'Today went so smoothly. I know that takes a lot of hard work and organisation.'

She flushed a little and that had a direct effect on Caius's body. He fought to control himself.

She said, 'I have a good team and your staff were helpful.'

Caius had also let it be known that if they'd needed any funds they could name their price but Poppy had favoured an economical wedding.

'It wasn't that I didn't want to be here to help—'

Poppy made an audibly disbelieving sound and Caius pulled her closer. The flush in her cheeks deepened and her eyes widened. Something surged inside him. Maybe she wasn't so immune after all.

He said, 'This marriage is a consequence of both our actions. I might be reluctant but you'd already vetoed me as a contender so I think we can call quits on where we both stand on that issue.'

Now Poppy looked uncomfortable. 'That's fair.'

'And the reason I wasn't here was because I had a financial situation to deal with.'

'A financial situation.' Poppy sounded unimpressed.

'Something I'd invested in lost funding.'

Now she looked unimpressed. 'I hope that when your son or daughter is born you'll recognise what is more important.'

She was assuming he'd prioritised making money over being present for the wedding preparations. Caius found himself in the familiar position of being judged—he'd be the first to admit that generally people had good reason to judge him, but not in this instance.

He could defend himself but something was cautioning him against it. As if he wasn't quite ready yet to beg for her approval. Because this whole situation and the currents flowing between them were something he'd never navigated before. So it was easier to let her believe the worst.

Instead he asked, 'So, Poppy…why that name? It's not exactly…regal, is it?'

She smiled sweetly and it almost distracted Caius from noticing that it didn't reach her eyes. 'Don't you mean it's more suited to an art student?'

Caius's conscience pricked hard again to think of her overhearing that conversation. He had been less than kind. 'You didn't deserve that.'

She looked a little surprised and then she shrugged minutely and said, 'My father was so sure that he would have a son to inherit the crown that he told my mother to call me whatever she wanted, so she did. She called me Poppy because it was her favourite flower and to annoy him, but it backfired when he had no objection to it.'

Caius stopped dancing and looked down at her. There was such a multitude of information in that breezily delivered answer that he wasn't sure what to unpick first. It made her solo walk down the aisle at the wedding even more poignant now.

She looked around and back at him, saying behind a fixed smile, 'Why have you stopped dancing?'

Because for some reason he'd felt a rush of anger at her father. Caius started dancing again. 'He married a few times, didn't he?'

Poppy nodded. 'Four times. Always in search of the elusive male heir.'

'That's why you had to marry to be crowned queen.'

She went a little pale. Caius cursed silently. 'Poppy, I can already see that you've made a positive impact on Valdere, even before you got married. He was obviously too blinkered to see what an asset you were.' Caius might have said something a lot more blunt and rude but he didn't want to offend her.

She looked up at him, cheeks going pink. 'I…thank you for saying that.'

Caius was momentarily mesmerised by her huge eyes and how they were glowing. He was forgetting that because of her father's archaic rule, and Caius's moment of weakness, they were now locked into this situation. But somehow, the necessary ire didn't feel as potent.

'You were here, living with him through each marriage?'

She nodded again. 'I was in boarding school for most of the year and then I used to visit my mother sometimes in upstate New York where she lives. Then I was in university in America.'

Even though she'd managed to escape these four walls Caius could well imagine what that must have been like when she had been here. He knew what a goldfish bowl it was to live in a royal palace. Everyone watching. No privacy. People looking at her every time her father failed to sire another child and moved on to another woman.

'If it's any consolation, I grew up being that coveted golden heir and it didn't work out so well for me, either.'

The music stopped at that moment and everyone clapped and cheered. Caius blinked and looked around. He'd actually forgotten for a moment about the crowd around them.

The guests were coming onto the dance floor to join them. Caius spied Cassie and Ares and even though Poppy had met them in passing earlier he introduced them properly now. Cassie shook Poppy's hand, smiling. 'From one queen to another, welcome to the small club.'

Caius noticed how stiff Poppy was but she seemed to relax under Cassie's sunny warmth. Not many could resist his sister. Certainly not his best man, Ares, who had a protective arm around Cassie now. Something Caius was still trying to get his head around.

'Thank you, and congratulations on your engagement.'

Cassie smiled even wider and grinned cheekily at Caius. 'I really didn't have my beloved brother getting married before me, *and* becoming a king again, on my bingo card for this year but he never fails to surprise.'

Caius glared at his sister to shut her up and said, 'King consort, Cass, not king.'

He felt Poppy's surprised glance at him. Obviously she'd not expected him to be happy to take a back seat in this relationship. But considering how her father had fought so hard for a son, maybe he could understand her expecting a male to want to dominate.

Except when he thought of domination now, all he could think of was of dominating Poppy in a much more basic and carnal way. Not that she would let him dominate her. She hadn't that first night. It had been an electric dance. And he wanted to dance with her again.

His resentment of this whole situation wasn't proving to be much of a deterrent.

An aide stepped forward and spoke into Poppy's ear. She looked at Caius. 'We can leave now.'

Relief swept through him to think of getting away from under all of these eyes. His sister's cheeky grin, as much as he loved her.

He kissed his sister on the cheek. 'Talk to you soon, Cass.' He looked at his friend and said sternly, 'Take care of her.'

'Always,' responded Ares, not even looking at Caius. Looking at his fiancée with an expression of such protectiveness and naked emotion that it made Caius feel like a voyeur and also something much more uncomfortable. A kind of wistfulness that freaked the hell out of him.

He turned away and he and Poppy followed the aide

out of the ballroom while everyone clapped and raised their glasses to the newly-weds.

Once outside the ballroom, Caius undid the top button of his dress jacket. Stephen was waiting and he looked at them with a smile on his face. 'Your things have been packed. The boat is ready.'

Caius's fingers dropped from his throat. 'Wait, what boat? Where are we going?'

Poppy turned to him. 'To the island in the lake. It's tradition for royal newly-weds to go there for the first few nights. It was in the information we sent you and you never objected so…'

Caius had a vague memory of his assistant in New York handing him a folder, saying, 'This is all the wedding information,' but that had been at the height of the financial snafu and Caius had just pushed it aside.

'First *few* nights? What does that mean?'

'It's to give us a chance to be seen to…' She trailed off.

Caius put up his hand. 'I get it.' To be seen to be honeymooning. So when the pregnancy was announced within the next few days, it could be believable they'd conceived out of genuine affection. To perpetuate some myth.

But all Caius could think about was that he hadn't really considered what would happen at all and he'd somehow believed that he'd be able to just get on a plane again and leave. But now it would appear he was to be incarcerated on an island.

'A few days, nights, is that really necessary?' Caius sent an explicit glance down to her belly and back up. 'We both know the deed is done.'

Poppy gritted out, ‘The people don’t know that.’

‘I was hoping to get back to New York.’ Even as he said that he heard how cold it sounded, but for some reason when he was around this woman she brought out the very worst in him.

Poppy’s eyes flashed. They were very green, distracting Caius momentarily. She said through visibly clenched teeth, ‘We have to be seen to be spending *some* time together. There is Internet connection on the island and I can assure you it’s exceedingly comfortable. Staff have already set up an office space for you. There’s a gym and a media room. A fully stocked library. It really shouldn’t be that onerous.’

Even Caius was smart enough to know to not give anyone fuel to start rumours. He had to think of his child, after all. The only reason he was doing this. *Really?* asked a little voice. Caius ignored it as he ignored the desire to take Poppy to a private space and unpeel all that lace and satin from her body. That was what had got them into this mess.

‘Fine. Let’s go.’

CHAPTER FIVE

POPPY DIDN'T KNOW why she'd allowed Caius's eagerness to leave Valdere again so soon to affect her. She wasn't calling it hurt. It couldn't be that. It was irritation. Anger, that he wasn't willing to give up his time for a honeymoon, to shore up this facade that it was a real marriage. That he hadn't even read over the information her team had sent him.

But for a moment when they'd been dancing and talking with surprising ease she'd almost forgotten about where they were and how many people were watching them avidly. His observation about what she'd done already for Valdere and her father being blinkered had impacted her deeply.

It was as if they'd taken two steps forward and one back again.

She couldn't help but admit to being disappointed at the evidence of his selfishness—focusing more on his money than his future child. She knew exactly the kind of person he was—she'd seen it first-hand and had the baby bump to prove it!

She couldn't afford to forget he was the master seducer—it was obviously so ingrained he couldn't help himself even with someone he didn't like.

She liked his sister. She seemed down-to-earth, friendly. And the interplay between her and Caius had caught at Poppy's chest because she'd seen genuine brother/sister affection. It reminded her of how lonely she'd always felt as an only child.

And the way things were working out, her child was destined to be another only child. Unless she followed her father's footsteps and remarried after Caius shook himself free of this marriage, the prospect of which there was zero doubt in Poppy's mind.

The island in the lake was a short boat ride from Valdere harbour. There were just a few buildings on the island—the chateau and a church and outbuildings that housed the caretaking staff and seasonal workers who tended the vines that grew on one side of the small island. They made a modestly good dessert wine from the vines.

Tourists came to visit for day trips and there was a cafe but it would be shut while they were in residence.

The boat came to a stop at the small island jetty and Caius got out and held out his hand to Poppy. She wanted to scowl and tell him he didn't have to bother pretending, it was just them and the staff now. But she took his hand and tried to ignore the little shiver of awareness as his fingers closed over hers and he pulled her onto the small jetty.

She felt ridiculous in the wedding dress now and cursed Clotilde for persuading her to leave it on—clearly the woman had romantic delusions, or maybe

Poppy had an illicit fantasy of Caius removing it on their wedding night?

A runaround golf buggy and driver were waiting for them. The staff had arrived ahead of them with their bags. Poppy couldn't wait to sink into a hot bath and try and pretend today hadn't happened. And that she didn't have to face days of looking at Caius's stony expression, no doubt as he was counting down the minutes until he could escape again.

In the back of the buggy as it was driven up the winding road to the castle, Caius asked, 'So what is this place?'

'One of my ancestors built it. A great-great-grandfather. Apparently he built it for his mistress, uncaring of the fact that his wife, the queen, could see it every time she looked out of the window of the palace. Since then, my ancestors have reclaimed it and tried to sanitise its less than savoury history by making a tradition of using it for the newly-wed king and queens.'

'Call me old-fashioned,' Caius drawled, 'but the Caribbean would be more my cup of tea for a honeymoon.'

Poppy had to admit that the thought of hot sun and translucent clear water and a white sand beach bordered by lush jungle sounded pretty idyllic too. She could envisage Caius lounging on the sand, droplets of seawater on his dark golden body, a beautiful woman sliding her leg between his while a sleek yacht floated just offshore.

Her imagination mocked her and she turned to Caius and said with faux sweetness, 'Haven't you heard? The cold-water swimming our lake provides is far more benefical to your health.'

Caius made a sound halfway between a snort and a grunt. 'I'll have to get back to you on that.'

Great, now she had just as provocative images of him hauling himself out of the lake onto the rocks, muscles bulging.

The buggy came to a stop at the front of the chateau. It never failed to make Poppy's breath catch. In the gathering dusk it looked even more magical, floodlit and with soft light coming out of the windows. Ever since she'd been young it had always looked to her like a fairy-tale castle *should* look, even if it more resembled a grand country house.

The fairy-tale bit of it was a round building with a turret roof on one end. The stone could look almost pink on some days and then, as the evening drew in, it turned golden.

But she wasn't in a fairy tale. She was here on her wedding night with a man who would prefer to be anywhere else. Any last hope that she'd ever secretly clung onto that things could be different for her had just died a death.

Staff were waiting at the open door and they were ushered inside. The housekeeper greeted them warmly and said, 'We've prepared a light supper if you're hungry?'

Poppy smiled at the woman who had taken care of this place for as long as she could remember. 'Thank you, Maud. I might eat something after I've changed and had a bath.'

'Of course, Your Highness. Chiara will go with you to your room to help you.'

Apparently even the housekeeper could read the situation and understand that the new king consort wouldn't be helping her to undress. For a moment Poppy felt intensely self-conscious. Exposed. She pushed it down. She had nothing to feel exposed about. She was doing the right thing. Giving her child legitimacy and a chance to know its father. As reluctant as he was. And at least for now, he was doing his part. The bare minimum, it had to be said. But it was better than nothing.

After the chateau's *mistress* era, the master bedroom suite in the tower had been reconfigured into two interconnecting bedrooms with separate bathrooms and dressing rooms. As if things had to swing in a much more puritanical way to compensate for the licentiousness of her adulterous ancestor.

So now, at least, it meant that she and Caius could keep their distance. Poppy overheard Caius asking Stephen to show him to the office to check up on some work. Then he turned to her and must have seen the slightly dumbfounded expression on her face because he asked, 'What? I don't think a consummation of this marriage is necessary.'

Poppy's face flamed. Had she imagined him asking her if she wanted to pick up where they'd left off in his office in New York? It would seem so. Obviously that had just been a well-worn reflex.

'I know it's not necessary, believe me.'

He looked at her and then said, 'Ah, you didn't expect me to want to work, is that it? You thought I'd be calling for a helicopter to take me to the nearest nightclub?'

Now Poppy felt like squirming. 'No, not exactly. I know you won't leave the island.'

'God forbid.' He sounded so bitter that it caught Poppy in that vulnerable place and she couldn't help asking, 'Is it really that bad? You being married? Becoming a king? Even when it was what you'd prepared for your whole life?'

All the staff had melted away and it was just them in the reception hall. A pregnant bride and her very unwilling groom who had the audacity to look not weary at all, but vital and far too gorgeous for Poppy's oversensitive hormones.

Caius dragged a hand through his hair, leaving it messy and even sexier. Poppy wanted to scowl.

Eventually he said, 'Look, I know that this wasn't your plan either. However it would still have been your path with someone else, if not me. But I'd been released from that obligation. As much as I didn't appreciate the circus around finding out I wasn't the king's son, I was free, for a moment, and only someone like you can appreciate what that means. I also liked the fact that I no longer had the responsibility of having a child for one purpose only, to serve. I won't ever regret my background, it was incredibly privileged, but it was never a choice.'

The problem was that Poppy could understand very well what Caius was saying, and empathise. And only for the fact that she hadn't had a brother to inherit the crown, she could have tasted that freedom too.

She put her hand on her belly. 'We can't change our pasts. I know the circumstances weren't ideal but I want this child, and I will love him, or her. They will never be made to feel like they've been born for one purpose, or that they have no choice. I know you feel like you're not here by choice, but you did choose to sacrifice your freedom for this child. You did the right thing.'

A short while later, on the balcony just beyond the French doors of the book-lined room where Poppy's staff had set up a working office for him, Caius looked into the inky darkness broodingly. At first he would have denied Poppy's words that he'd had a choice in anything to do with this situation, but she was right.

He could have turned his back on her and denied any involvement until the baby was born and had paternity proved. But he also knew he couldn't have. Because no matter what kind of a devil-may-care persona he'd cultivated, he'd never really erred too far from what was acceptable.

He wasn't a monster. He wouldn't have put Poppy in that position under intense public scrutiny and judgement.

He'd been a playboy, yes. But he'd never lost control of his senses. Never done drugs. And as for women, he'd slept with his fair share, no denying that, but about one per cent of the actual number the tabloids would have people believe, and he'd never ever let a woman think that there was anything more to it than sex.

If they'd cried foul, and many had, it had only been to try and extort something out of Caius.

And, perhaps even more crucially, Caius had believed Poppy about the baby.

When he thought about that night in Paris with the benefit of hindsight, the signs had been there that she'd been a virgin. He'd just been too hot for her to notice them. But she'd been shy. A little awkward. *And tight.* His body responded now to that memory and how the strength of her orgasm had made him see stars.

He'd always found sex enjoyable but not…so mind-bendingly explosive that he'd passed out. *It had been because she was a virgin,* assured a little voice. But Caius wasn't so sure. Because he still wanted her. He wanted to know if it would be the same again. More intense? Most likely less.

One thing he was sure of was that if he had Poppy again, her appeal would soon fade. It always did.

She might be trying to fool him or even herself that she didn't want him, but he felt the hum of electricity between them. Felt the crackle if they got too close. She'd been melting against him when they'd danced earlier and they'd both lost track of where they were.

He'd always known not to expect to *want* his royal wife. And yet here he was, aching for his very royal and very unexpected wife.

At that moment a light came on above Caius's head and up to his right-hand side where the bedrooms were situated in the tower. He looked up and held his breath when he saw Poppy step out onto a terrace that ran around that part of the building.

Her hair was down in loose waves and she was changed out of the wedding dress and into what looked like a silk strappy vest top and matching shorts. Shorts with slits in the sides, showing off her toned thighs. Thighs he could remember gripping his hips tight. The memory of her breathless entreaties filled his head. *More, harder...please.*

She ran her hands through her hair, obviously massaging her skull, and the dark auburn glinted in the soft golden light coming from the room behind her.

The breeze pressed her top against her breasts, outlining their full shape, and then it lifted, exposing her belly and the gentle firm swell. Without his even realising what he was doing, Caius's hands had gone to the wall and he was holding on tight because the world felt as if it were spinning a little.

She put her hands on her belly, either side, and was looking down, an expression of absorption on her face. Something pierced the tide of hot desire engulfing Caius. It took him a second to realise it was envy, that he wasn't the one inspiring that level of absorption.

Jealous of his own unborn child? Caius ducked back into the office again quickly before Poppy might catch him ogling her like a lusty teenager. He saw a drinks cabinet in the corner of the room and went over, pouring himself a measure of whiskey, throwing it back, hoping that it might help eclipse the raging need inside him.

It didn't. Caius knew fatefully that nothing would quench it except indulging it. He wanted his wife. How very inconvenient when there was a mountain of baggage between them.

And yet…they were here on this island, albeit within swimming distance of Valdere City, for the next few days, for all intents and purposes to create a child that was already growing within her womb.

And Caius really did have to come to terms with this whole situation because it wasn't going to end any time soon. So instead of fighting it…maybe he should just go with the flow a little and get to know his new wife. It had never been in his nature to invite conflict, not after watching his parents tear emotional lumps out of each other all his life.

He couldn't deny that Poppy wasn't like his other women. But that didn't mean that things would be any different once he'd had her again. It wasn't as if it would go any deeper than the physical anyway. Even if she was the mother of his child. A concept, he had to admit uncomfortably, that was becoming more and more real in a way he hadn't anticipated.

He pictured her again with her hands either side of that small but very definite bump, skin glowing pale in the moonlight. He pushed that image and revelation aside.

All he wanted was the physical. And if there was one thing he excelled at, it was seducing women.

The following morning Poppy was sitting on the outdoor terrace being served breakfast. It would be another beautiful clear sunny day. She could hear the gentle lap of the lake water meeting the rocky shore at the end of the garden, where it sloped gently downwards.

She was at the back of the chateau and so faced a spectacular view of the mountains. It was peaceful and quiet and for a moment she could almost forget that she was now a married woman. A queen. With a king.

A king who was still in bed apparently. And she'd slept late—unintentionally—a side effect from the long day before. She blamed pregnancy hormones.

But then for a sybarite like Caius Mansur, sleeping late was probably quite usual.

The newspapers were spread on the table, brought over from the mainland first thing. Pictures of her kiss with Caius on the palace balcony was on the cover of almost every tabloid and broadsheet.

Poppy picked up the nearest paper, taking in the photo and the way Caius's hand was on her jaw. She was leaning towards him, one hand lifted and fingers spread across his chest. How had she let it be so...provocative? It looked undeniably sexual. Was it just the effect of this man? That everything he looked at and touched somehow became more erotic?

Suddenly a bit breathless, she looked away from the photo to the printed words of the article. But she stopped skim-reading when something caught her eye and found herself reading intently.

'Good morning.'

Poppy looked up from the article and her eyes widened on a bare-chested Caius, who was wet, and dripping water onto the terrace. He had a small towel slung around his slim hips and it took a second for Poppy's brain to function, so unexpected was this vision.

Before she could stop herself she blurted out, 'I thought you were still in bed.' Far from it. He was wide awake and glowing with rude vitality, body honed and muscular.

One dark brow arched. 'I've been up since six a.m., and you're right, the lake was extremely refreshing.'

Oof. She was the one just out of bed in leggings and a loose T-shirt. No make-up. Hair pulled back into a careless bun. Even though he was half naked, she felt like the untidy one.

'I didn't know you wore glasses,' he observed.

Poppy reached for them, taking them off. She didn't wear contacts when she was considered off duty. Feeling prickly, she said, 'Well, it's not as if we've spent a whole lot of time around each other.'

His gaze flicked to her mid-section and back up and he said dryly, 'We've spent enough time together.'

She felt that like a little sharp dart. Another reminder of why they were here and how she'd curtailed his life.

Caius sat down on the other side of the table and staff attended him, bringing fresh fruit, granola, pastries, coffee. He smiled and thanked them. Poppy couldn't seem to take her gaze off his chest, broad and muscled. The smattering of dark hair, curling wetly against his skin. The dark discs of his nipples. It was positively indecent.

She lifted her gaze and he was watching her, those blue eyes far too bright and knowing. Nothing wrong with her eyesight now. She could feel a blush rising upwards and took a quick sip of tea to try and stave it off.

When they were alone again, he said, sounding amused, 'I suppose I shouldn't be surprised you thought I was still in bed.'

She couldn't stop the blush this time but he seemed to take pity on her, saying, 'The truth is that I've always been an early bird. Even with a hangover.'

This sat a little uneasily now with what she'd just read in the paper. Caius flicked a glance down. 'Anything of interest?'

Poppy put the paper down. 'Why didn't you tell me the full story about the financial crisis you were dealing with?'

Caius took a sip of coffee, unconcerned. 'I didn't think you were interested.'

'You let me think the worst.'

'*I* didn't do anything. If you came to that conclusion that was on you.'

He had a point, damn him. And then he seemed to take pity on her, saying with a shrug, 'I'm used to people thinking the worst. It doesn't bother me.'

Poppy didn't believe that for a second. No one was that immune to criticism. 'You don't exactly help the situation.'

Caius's gaze narrowed on her. 'I learnt a long time ago that the media like to stick to a certain narrative, and I'm not saying I didn't give them the ammunition, but it grew bigger than me, and if I'd gone up against them, it would have created an even bigger storm.'

Poppy snorted a little. 'So you're saying it was all lies?'

'Not all, no, but about twenty per cent of what they reported had some truth.'

Poppy lifted up the paper. 'And this?'

Now Caius looked a little uncomfortable. 'True.'

Poppy assimilated that. The fact that Caius's financial crisis had actually been something not so superficial at all. A tech company he'd invested in had almost gone bust due to losing state funding, potentially causing mass unemployment in a small town in Southern Italy. Caius had stepped in, using his own finances to prop it up until the government had restored that funding.

'Don't look at me like that, Poppy.'

'Like what?'

'I'm not suddenly some white knight. I saved that business because I had a stake in it. It made sense.'

The fact that he'd single-handedly turned that situation around and saved hundreds of jobs in a challenged region struggling to invest in new technology as a long-term initiative might indeed make sense, but Poppy suspected the human aspect had played a bigger role than he would admit. And that was intriguing.

He peeled a small orange and asked, 'So, are you going to give me a tour of the island?'

A little taken aback she asked, 'You want to spend time with me?'

He shrugged. 'I figure maybe it's time for a little truce. After all, we're married now and will become parents in about five months' time. We're on an island. What else is there to do?'

Was there a gleam in his eyes or was that her imagination? Why did Poppy suddenly feel as if the rules had been changed? And as if the earth had just tilted on its axis slightly? As though the man she'd thought she had summed up was suddenly not the sum of those parts at all, but something entirely unexpected? And why did that make her feel so nervous?

Because something *had* just changed. And it was dangerous because she knew well that, contrary to what she'd told herself about that night in Paris—that the sex hadn't been about emotion—it had in fact been all about emotion. Because Caius had got to her that night, under her skin. She'd trusted him enough to sleep with him.

She'd obviously sensed something more to him.

He'd touched a place inside her where she protected herself against rejection and abandonment. He'd made her feel wanted and desired and seen. And that was terrifying. And why she'd called off the engagement discussions.

Yet here she was. Carrying his child. Married. For at least five years. She couldn't let him see that she still wanted him. It was more important than ever to keep boundaries intact or she'd never get through this. In any case, she didn't have to worry about him throwing her over his shoulder to take her to bed. He couldn't have made it clearer last night that he had no interest in her.

Once they were through this mandatory honeymoon period she would be encouraging him to go back to

New York or wherever he wanted to go. She could get on with ruling her people as she wanted to, ushering in a new era. She hated the little prick of regret that she'd be doing it on her own but this was the consequence of her choices.

He smiled. 'You can trust me, I promise.'

Poppy sent him a look. Of one thing she was still certain: she couldn't trust this man as far as she could throw him. But she wasn't about to let him see how unnerved she was.

She forced a bright smile and said, 'I'll get changed and we'll head out.'

CHAPTER SIX

'YOU CAN DRIVE, you know the place.'

Caius was indicating for Poppy to take the wheel of the runaround buggy. She was annoyed with herself for automatically assuming he would want to drive. Her father had always told her she was too independent and that men didn't like it.

She got in behind the wheel. She'd dressed down in cut-off shorts that still fitted her if she left the top button open, and a loose linen shirt. Slip-on sneakers, because some of the terrain could be rocky.

She tried not to be too aware of Caius's muscular thigh close to hers. He was casual too, wearing long shorts and a polo shirt in light blue that she didn't have to look to know would enhance his eyes. Thankfully he was wearing shades, like her.

They set off on the main road and Poppy pointed out various sights. The small church.

Caius asked, 'Was anyone ever married there?'

Poppy shook her head. 'Not in recent history. It was the first dwelling on the island though, so we think maybe it was used in medieval times. It dates back that far. Want to have a look?'

'Sure.'

Poppy stopped the buggy and they got out. The doors to the small church weren't locked and she pushed them open, revealing the small, hushed interior. Musky and dusty. It was simple inside. Plain. About four rows of pews on either side and an altar.

Caius seemed to easily dominate the space with his broad shoulders and height. He wandered in, looking around, and up at the vaulted ceiling.

In a bid to stop herself staring at him, Poppy said, 'This must be quite the change from your usual haunts.'

He'd pushed his glasses on top of his head, like her, and he looked at her. She groaned inwardly. Yes, she could confirm that his eyes were even more ridiculously blue wearing that shirt.

'I actually like churches.'

Poppy nearly tripped over her own feet. 'Sorry, what?'

He gave a half-rueful smile. 'I had, well, that is, Cassie and I had an Irish nanny for a while. Cassie was only a baby. I was about five. Her name was Mary, and she was very religious and she used to go into churches to light candles all the time. I found the churches… peaceful. Probably because my parents were always arguing, so they felt somewhat comforting.'

Intrigued by this snippet, she said, 'Your, um, parents didn't get on?' There'd been rumours about the king and queen of Sadat Sur Mer and their acrimonious relationship, but when Poppy had been younger she'd tuned out gossip among the palace staff. She wished she'd listened more now.

Caius shook his head, his expression visibly closing a little. 'They despised each other but for the main the public perception was that they were blissfully in love. Everyone wants to believe in a fairy tale.' The bitterness in Caius's voice was evident.

He continued, 'It was only palace insiders and staff and some other royal circles who knew the truth. From as far back as I can remember, they argued, over every little thing. It didn't help that my mother flaunted her affairs under my father's nose. And then he would return the favour.'

Poppy's heart constricted. 'That wasn't very nice.'

'No, they weren't very nice people.'

It was almost refreshing to hear someone describe their parents like that. Poppy found herself saying, 'My father didn't have affairs but he kept marrying to try and have the son he wanted. Needless to say that didn't make for good relationships.'

'Why didn't he have any more children?'

Poppy shrugged. 'I remember a fight he had with my mother shortly before they split up where she was telling him her tests had come back fine so the problem must be his. I didn't understand it at the time but I figure my father obviously became infertile for some reason.'

Poppy realised that she'd never told anyone else that and suddenly became aware of how intimate the space was in the small building. Caius had told her to trust him and here she was spilling her guts ten minutes later. She was pathetic. 'Shall we keep going?'

'Lead the way,' Caius said, putting out a hand indicating for her to precede him out of the church. Like that first night they'd met, it struck her that he was courteous, polite. Not traits associated with selfish playboys. What he'd said came back to her: *About twenty per cent of what they reported was true.* Still, considering the life he'd led, twenty per cent of bedding beautiful women and frequenting the world's most glittering nightclubs and bars and parties was still more than the average human would ever experience.

But that knowledge pricked under her skin like a little burr as they got back into the buggy and went on with their tour around the island. She had to acknowledge that there was more to him than—

'You're thinking so hard I can hear you.'

Poppy almost veered off the road but Caius put a hand to the wheel, steadying it. 'OK?'

Poppy nodded. She was mortified that Caius had witnessed her overthinking *him*, literally as he was beside her. She decided to articulate her thoughts. 'Why finance? When presumably you didn't have to work at all?'

She glanced at him and back to the road. Eventually he answered, 'I was never comfortable with the thought of doing nothing—aside from my duties as a crown prince. I was always good at numbers, they made sense to me. I interned in the City of London after university and started building my own investment business.'

Poppy frowned, taking a corner carefully, as the road started to climb. 'I don't recall reading about the internship in your bio.'

Caius shifted beside her and stretched out his arm behind her along the seat. Poppy's skin tingled and she had to concentrate hard on driving.

He said, 'I kept it low-key, didn't broadcast my title. A few people knew but they soon lost interest. They only cared if I could manage clients' portfolios. It lasted at least until the media got wind of what I was doing and that…was the end of that. I had to leave.'

Poppy heard a thread of weariness in his voice. She guessed his days of being crowned as Europe's most eligible royal bachelor must have started around then.

'What did you do in university?' he asked.

'International relations and political science.' She felt staid even as she said that. She made a face. 'Not exactly inspired.'

'Was it what you wanted to do?'

'Not especially, but my father put pressure on me. There was an English Literature and Theatre Studies class I would have loved to do.'

'You wanted to be an actress?'

No doubt he thought her far too boring. 'Is that so hard to believe?'

She saw him shake his head in her peripheral vision. 'No, not at all. The woman I saw in the photo… maybe, but not you.'

A bloom of heat filled her solar plexus. Poppy had often thought of herself as employing acting skills to avoid showing her father how much he hurt her. And maybe she'd called on it too the night she'd met Caius in Paris, convincing herself she could step out of her comfort zone.

But here she was now, and no acting in the world could hide the vulnerability Caius seemed to make her feel.

She admitted, 'My father commissioned that photo before he died. I hated it. It wasn't me.'

They emerged now through the trees at the top of a hill. Poppy brought the buggy to a halt and got out. Caius stepped out too and looked at her. 'Why did you let him dim your light?'

Poppy squirmed a little. How could she explain, without seeming weak, that a part of her had still craved her father's approval in spite of the constant rejection? And then, as if he was able to read her mind, he said, 'Actually…when it comes to parents and behaving in ways to either gain or provoke attention, I can't exactly talk. I made a career out of courting the media partly in order to get my parents' attention. Not that it worked.'

Poppy felt a burst of affinity and gratitude for his understanding. Gratefully she changed the subject. 'This gives you an overview of the whole island, and Valdere.'

Caius stood beside her, looking around him. 'It's beautiful. I don't think I've been somewhere so peaceful in a long time.'

Before she could stop herself she was saying, 'Don't you mean boring? I'm sure you're dying to get back to the city and a hectic social life.'

The thought of that world felt very far away and Caius realised he had no desire for it. He shook his head, 'Actually…not so much.' What he did desire was much closer. He looked at Poppy and a breeze flattened her shirt against her belly. 'Your bump looks bigger today.'

Poppy put a hand on it and huffed a little laugh. 'I think the baby is having a growth spurt after the constriction of the dress yesterday.'

'Can you feel anything yet?'

'Little flutters, like butterflies inside. It feels strange.'

'You look…good.' She looked amazing. Sexy.

Poppy looked up at Caius a little suspiciously. 'I… thank you, I feel good. No sickness, thankfully.' She took a step back. 'We should probably get back. I can show you the vineyard on the way.'

But Caius caught her arm before she could turn away and she looked up at him.

'I mean, you look really good, Poppy. I saw you last night on your balcony. I didn't mean to…'

She frowned. 'What are you saying, Caius?'

He faced her directly now, his hand still on her arm but in such a gentle hold she could have pulled away. She didn't.

'I still want you, Poppy. I haven't been with anyone else since that night in Paris. You left an impression.'

Her green eyes widened and her cheeks went pink. But then, like watching storm clouds race across a clear sky, her expression darkened and her eyes narrowed. She pulled back. 'You are unbelievable.'

He frowned. 'What are you talking about?'

'We're on an island…you said it yourself, and you're so highly sexed that you figure you'll sleep with the only convenient female around to get through the boredom, is that it?'

Caius was indignant. '*No!* That is not it. I'm not that desperate for sex, believe me.'

'So I'm supposed to be flattered?'

He gritted his jaw and then said, 'You're supposed to be honest and admit you want me too. It's obvious, Poppy.'

The pink in her cheeks deepened, which had an incendiary effect on Caius's desire. She said loftily, 'Not every woman is in thrall to you, Caius.'

'I don't want every woman, I just want you, more's the pity.'

'Charming.'

They were both breathing heavily and glaring at each other. Poppy blurted out then, 'Are you telling the truth about not being with anyone else?'

Exposure skated over Caius's skin but he said, 'Why would I lie?'

Normally this would be anathema to him—giving any woman cause to read anything more into his desire for her than what it was: just physical attraction. But this was different. They were married. She was having his baby. They'd already transgressed about a million boundaries he was usually rigid about.

As if to make sure there was no ambiguity he said, 'It doesn't mean anything more than the fact that we have powerful chemistry. That's all.'

Poppy hated that that stung a little—that he felt he had to remind her this had nothing to do with emotions. But then, did she want emotions involved? With a man like Caius—a renowned commitment phobe? Someone who had rejection of his lovers built into his DNA? No way.

And yet the way he'd asked her how she'd let her father dim her light had touched her—his perspicacity. But then, all that meant was that he was a good observer of people. He didn't *care*.

He looked so serious now that she had to concede that he wasn't someone who needed to lie to get a woman into bed. All he'd had to do to seduce her in the first place was to take off his shirt.

So it hadn't just been a platitude in New York when he'd told her he wanted to see her again. Before she'd told him she was pregnant. When he'd still thought it would just be an affair.

But she couldn't afford to forget the reason she'd shut down discussions around a marriage had been because of how she'd reacted to him that night. Wanton and totally uninhibited. She'd effectively rejected him before he could reject her. Because he'd got too close.

'I don't think that's a good idea, Caius. You don't really want me, it's just convenient now.'

'I never stopped wanting you.'

'Until I told you I was pregnant and that we'd have to marry,' she pointed out.

Caius shook his head. 'No, I wanted you even then, but I was in shock. Do I need to remind you that first of all I had no idea who you were, and the second time we met you told me you were pregnant. Within twenty-four hours of that we were having engagement pictures taken in Central Park and then we didn't meet again until yesterday.'

'Exactly, we barely know each other.'

'And yet we were making love within an hour of meeting one another for the first time.'

'But you hate me now.'

'I don't hate you, Poppy. I don't hate anyone. It's a waste of time. I saw what hate does to people with my parents and it's corrosive and toxic.'

She wondered if that was why Caius had pushed out the need to select a suitable partner for as long as possible. After all, she'd kept people at arm's length for fear of being rejected.

You didn't keep him at arm's length. No, because she'd thought she'd been safe, and that she'd never see him again.

'You don't want to be here,' she reminded him.

His mouth tipped up minutely on one side. 'I think that horse has bolted. I'm here.'

'Last night you said it wasn't as if we had to consummate the marriage…'

Caius made a face. 'I think I was trying to deny that I still wanted you. It's not usual for me to feel an attraction like this…and especially not with the added complication of our situation. I'm not saying this now because it's convenient, Poppy. It'd be a lot more convenient if I didn't want you and I could just get on with—'

'Sleeping with other women?' Poppy blurted out hotly.

Caius looked at her. 'I like sex, Poppy. I like women. Not too close, admittedly, but I've never promised any lover more than I've been able to give. But yes, I'd assumed with any royal marriage that I'd keep the two things very separate. And I can be discreet when it suits me, believe it or not. I wouldn't have disrespected you as my father did my mother, as they did to each other.'

He continued, 'But this…situation—'

'We're married, it's not a situation,' Poppy inserted, still feeling prickly at the thought of him blithely seeking out his lovers. He'd agreed to a duration of five years for this marriage but there had been nothing in black and white about fidelity.

'OK, fine, this *marriage* has not conformed to any expectations I ever had. I want you, Poppy. I want my wife. But we both know where we stand here. There's no ambiguity. No promise of anything more.'

To Poppy's shame and consternation, she could feel herself weakening. Because she did want him too. She was desperate to know if it would feel the same. Be as good. As amazing. She'd believed he'd never touch her again, but he was looking at her now as if he was barely holding onto his restraint and it was seriously exciting.

Nevertheless, she tried to resist. 'What if I don't want you?'

Caius lifted his gaze from where it had been on her mouth. He said, 'I've never forced a woman in my life, and I'm not about to start. If you say you don't want me, I have to respect that. I won't touch a hair on your head.'

She believed him. In this, he had integrity. And he was proud. He wouldn't debase himself. But the thought of the next few days stretching out between them with this palpable tension between them and knowing that he wanted her… Poppy could feel herself caving.

That night with Caius in Paris had been the most reckless thing she'd ever done in her life. And they were here now, because of the consequences of that act. Would it be so bad to take something for herself again?

She felt acutely conscious of her own desire. She'd always imagined attraction and sex would be civilised matters, not this stomach-clenching, prickling, hot urgency under her skin, in her blood. It was animalistic.

Caius put his hands up now and took a step back. 'OK, fine, if you don't want this then I won't mention it again. Maybe you're right, things are complicated enough.'

But suddenly Poppy felt reckless again. This man wasn't rejecting her. He wanted her. He hadn't been with anyone else since her. He turned to walk back to the buggy and she turned and called out, 'Wait, stop.'

He stopped. Turned around.

A volcanic surge of need mixed with a kind of possessiveness she'd never experienced before propelled Poppy forward and her arms were around Caius's neck and he was stumbling backwards and wrapping his arms around her at the same time and just about managing to stay upright as Poppy breathed out, 'Damn you, Caius Mansur—' just before her mouth connected with his and she kissed him with a fervour born of everything roiling around inside her.

The fact that Caius matched that fervour, splaying

his big hands across her back and holding her to him, only made her press closer.

Their mouths were fused, Poppy's blood was pumping, heart clamouring. Then something shifted…became less desperate. Caius eased back slightly and said against her mouth, 'Take a breath, it's OK, we have all the time in the world.'

Poppy opened her mouth slightly and sucked in air and Caius's mouth settled on hers again and the desperation faded, to be replaced with something more languorous and toe-curlingly erotic.

His tongue stroked hers and heat pooled deep inside Poppy, between her legs. Her belly was pressed against Caius's body and she could feel his erection between them. She was practically climbing him like a tree. Everything around them forgotten.

After long drugging minutes, Poppy pulled back and looked up into Caius's face. His cheeks were flushed, eyes glittering. Hungry. The evidence of his desire made her feel a hundred and one things at once along with a pricking of insecurity—was this her unique effect on him or was this just his sexual frustration?—but she pushed it aside. She needed him too much. But she also needed to reiterate to herself that she had this under control.

'This is just physical, right?'

He nodded. 'It'll burn out. It always does.'

Somehow, Poppy didn't find that hugely reassuring but she was too hot for him to question it. 'We can see the vineyards another time. Let's go back to the chateau.'

Cauis took her hand and led her, on distinctly wobbly legs, back to the buggy and this time he got into the driver's seat. Poppy didn't care, she just wanted him to get them back to the chateau before she could overthink what was happening.

Caius drove carefully but fast and within minutes he was leading her into the chateau and to the wing with the bedrooms, and up the winding stairs and into his bedroom suite, which mirrored hers more or less exactly except for the decor. This suite was more muted, and neutral. But Poppy didn't see any of that. All she could see was Caius, commanding the space.

He stood apart from her and said, 'Undo your hair.'

She'd pulled her hair back into a loose ponytail. She reached back and pulled out the tie. The fact that he seemed to like her hair filled her with a sense of confidence. Her father used to look at her and say, 'No one in this family was ever a redhead, it must be from your mother's side.' It had been another strike against her. Another reason to not be good enough.

But Caius came forward now and reached for her hair, loosening it out and spreading it over her shoulders. She luxuriated in the sensation like a cat. Then he dropped his hands to her shirt and looked at her. 'OK?'

She nodded. He undid the buttons and pulled the shirt open. She immediately felt self-conscious. Her breasts were bigger and she'd all but forgotten about the belly, which now felt huge.

But Caius was looking at her, avid, cheeks flared with colour. Hesitantly, Poppy said, 'I'm a bit…bigger.'

Caius slid the shirt off her shoulders and down her arms and it fell to the floor.

'You are beautiful.'

She felt beautiful—as she'd felt beautiful on that first night. So to be here with him again, and considering all that had happened in the meantime, was a little overwhelming. To avoid thinking about it too much Poppy reached behind her and undid her bra, peeling it off and letting it drop to the floor.

Caius sucked in an audible breath and then said, *'Deus...'*

'What language is that?'

Caius's gaze was on her breasts, feasting on them. Poppy's nipples tightened with need. They were more tender.

'Hm?' Caius looked up.

'The…language…what you just said.'

'It's a mix…in Sadat, we've had so many influences that we have a dialect that's a mishmash of about four different languages.'

And then he arched a brow. 'I'm doing something wrong here if you're more interested in linguistics right now.'

A little burble of laughter broke free and Poppy said, 'No, it's me… I tend to go into my head when I'm feeling…a little overwhelmed.'

He took her hand and led her over to the bed. 'Well, let's get you out of your head, OK?'

'Yes, please.'

Poppy lay down and watched as Caius took off his shirt, revealing that glorious chest, and then he undid his shorts and pushed them down and off, with his underwear. He kicked off shoes and then came over and undid Poppy's shorts, pulling them down and off, along with her underwear, and then slid off her sneakers.

He looked at her for a long moment, eyes tracking over her body, and then he came down on the bed beside her.

'Kiss me, Caius...please.'

He lowered his head and covered her mouth with his and she arched against him, needing to feel his body on hers. In hers. But he was being careful. She pulled back. 'I'm not fragile, Caius...touch me, please.'

As if he'd needed her permission, he took her mouth again, hard, and then his hands were on her, tracing over her curves, her waist and the burgeoning bump of her belly, lingering there for a moment before moving up to cup her breasts. She pulled back a little and sucked in a breath.

He was looking at her. 'Did I do something?'

She shook her head. 'No, they're just a bit...tender.'

'I'll go gently, then, shall I?'

Caius looked at her as he lowered his head again but this time his mouth found her nipple and closed over it, teasing with his teeth and tongue, and Poppy's head nearly exploded at the sensation. It was torture. It was exquisite.

Then he was moving down and pressing kisses to her exposed skin, belly, hands shaping her as he moved, until he was at the juncture of her legs and pushing her thighs apart, rearing back a little so he could look at her.

Poppy felt so needy. 'Please, Caius…do something.' Pressure was building.

He obliged, coming down between her legs, and then everything went blurry when she felt his tongue on her, exploring the centre of her body in broad strokes, and then finding that little sensitive nub and sucking powerfully. It was all Poppy needed to fly, and she soared so high she was afraid she'd never return to earth, but she did, floating back to reality, her body clasping and pulsating with pleasure.

Caius was reaching for something—protection—and Poppy said, 'We don't need that, do we?'

He looked at her and then at her belly and smiled a little ruefully. 'No, I guess not. I'm clean, by the way, I had a check-up.'

Poppy felt shy. 'I've only been with you.'

Caius had never been in this situation before. He was pretty certain he'd never slept with a virgin because he'd always sought out women who were experienced and would know how to play the game.

Poppy had been the exception to that rule. And it was truly disturbing how satisfying it was to hear her say that he had been her only lover. So much so that Caius shelved that away to think about…never.

She was laid out before him, her body glowing after her orgasm, curvy…bountiful. And her belly, that small proud bump, under which grew his child. His seed. Caius had never expected to feel any kind of a connection with his child, or children, after growing up with parents who'd paid scant attention to him or his sister.

But this…got to him on a deeply primal level. Before he could let that thought grow roots and seriously freak him out, he obeyed the ravenous need of his body to be buried in this woman and he came down over her, careful to shield her from his full weight as he guided his cock to her entrance and almost came at the feel of her slick body.

He somehow managed not to explode and pushed inside, sweat breaking out on his brow as he sank in, deeper and deeper until he was buried to the hilt and her muscles were snug around him, like a hot silken sheath.

Merda. He'd never felt anything like it. Not even that first time had felt this good. He pulled back out again and watched Poppy's eyes get a little dazed. Her hands were on his hips, fingers digging in.

'You feel so good.' He couldn't keep the words back and normally he never spoke during sex.

'You feel…amazing, don't stop, Caius…'

He had no intention of it. He was in heaven and hell, simultaneously. The hell of needing to give into the urge to just explode and the heaven of eking out the pleasure so it would be even better.

He struck up a rhythm and felt Poppy's body move with him. Their skin was sheened with perspiration. The need to let go was gathering at the base of Caius's spine and drawing everything up tight, Poppy was biting her lip. She was close but he was going to come before her unless he did something, so he bent down and put his mouth over one straining nipple, sucking the flesh deep into his mouth and rolling it under his tongue.

He heard Poppy's cry just as she arched into him and the muscles of her vagina clamped so tight around him that he came in a torrent of ecstasy, his whole body jerking helplessly, losing all control or do anything but ride the wave.

In the aftershocks of pleasure, Caius extricated himself from Poppy's still-clasping body and slumped down beside her, instinctively pulling her close, a hand over her belly.

He wasn't going to think about the fact that normally after sex he couldn't get free fast enough. He was in no fit state to consider that now. All he could do was follow the dictates of his body and slide into a pleasure coma.

When Poppy woke it was dusk outside. She lifted her head, sensing immediately she was alone. She was practically spreadeagled on the bed, naked from the waist up, and the thought of Caius being somewhere nearby, coming back and finding her in this wanton state, had her pulling up the sheet like a blushing virgin.

She most definitely was not a virgin. She couldn't believe the day was practically gone. She remembered waking after they'd made love that first time, and, without words, they'd made love again, Caius taking Poppy from behind, lifting her leg, his hands full of her breasts, climaxing together within minutes. Fast and silent and intense.

And so from then…to now, she'd been unconscious. This time she was the one waking up and finding herself alone. As Caius would have if he hadn't caught her trying to steal out of that room in Paris.

She had to admit it didn't feel all that nice. She felt insecure. Wondering if she'd embarrassed herself by her responses. Had she been gauche? Had her inexperience been a turn-off? And she hadn't realised how much she'd like the way Caius had tucked her into him, curling his big body around hers, hands possessively on her breasts.

She'd never considered herself a very tactile person. Neither of her parents had been all that tactile and she'd instinctively avoided it all her life—another way to avoid rejection, don't seek contact!—so it was something of a surprise to find that she liked it.

A lot. Before she could think about that too much, she got up and saw her clothes placed neatly across the back of a chair. Had Caius done that? She couldn't imagine the staff would have intruded. Clutching her clothes to her, she went through the adjoining door that led into her suite and straight into the shower, tucking her hair up and out of the way.

After the shower she dithered over what to wear. What was this? What were they doing here? Apart, obviously, from doing what every other newly-wed couple did—but they weren't every other newly-wed couple. If it weren't for this crazy chemistry, no doubt they'd be at opposite ends of the chateau minding their own business.

A dark green colour caught Poppy's eye and she

reached for it. It was a silk maxi-dress, loose and flowing, high neck but sleeveless. Not too fancy. Not too casual. She pulled it on before she could obsess over it too much and brushed her hair out and put on a minimum of make-up. Wedge sandals. She tried not to think about how the silk felt next to her sensitised skin. It felt sensual. Sexy.

As she went down into the chateau she cursed herself for feeling apprehensive. Nervous. Like a teenager going on a date.

Some candles were lighting along the corridors but it was suspiciously quiet. Poppy suddenly realised she was ravenous and made her way down to the big open-plan rustic kitchen. Maybe Caius was in the office that had been set up for him?

She wasn't going to go looking for him like some— She stopped on the threshold of the kitchen. She didn't have to go looking for Caius because he was here. In worn jeans and a fresh T-shirt. Hair damp. Doing something at the cooker.

CHAPTER SEVEN

POPPY BLINKED BUT he was still there. Not a mirage. He turned around and Poppy couldn't stop her eyes widening on the way he filled out the T-shirt and jeans and the wooden spoon in his hand.

He said, 'I was going to wake you in a bit. Are you hungry?'

Poppy shook her head as if that might help make sense of the scenario she was facing. She saw Caius's frown and said, 'No, I mean, yes, I'm hungry, I just… hadn't expected to see you here. Like this.'

She walked in. Caius turned back to the pan, where something was sizzling and smelled amazing. Poppy's mouth watered. 'What is that?'

He turned to face her again. 'Steak. You're not a vegetarian, are you?'

'No.' Her belly rumbled and she blushed, hoping he hadn't heard. 'Where's Maud? And the chef?'

'I told Maud she and her staff could take the evening off. I hope you don't mind?'

She looked around and saw the massive wooden table that the staff used. Big bifold doors opened out onto the chateau walled garden where they grew their own vegetables. It was as idyllic a dinner scene as Poppy could have liked.

She sat on one of the high chairs placed around the massive kitchen island. ‘No. You cook?’

Caius made a face. ‘That’s a bit of a stretch. I can do a few basics, steak being one. And I’m a whizz at heating stuff up. Chef was kind enough to leave some ingredients. I’ve never particularly enjoyed being waited on.’

‘Me too,’ she admitted. ‘I was always so conscious that staff probably wanted to be anywhere else than watching me.’

Poppy couldn’t believe she’d let that slip out. Before Caius might reflect on it she jumped up and said, ‘Shall I set the table?’

‘Be my guest, you probably know where everything is.’

Poppy started to search for cutlery and napkins, saying, ‘Actually, I don’t. I used to come with my nanny when I was small. I think she was in love with someone working here and used me as an excuse to visit. But I haven’t been here in years.’

She didn’t say that she used to look out of the windows back towards the palace on the mainland and imagine that her parents were together and in love and that they were a real family.

‘So your parents didn’t use it as a love nest?’

Poppy let out an inadvertent laugh at that and pulled a couple of napkins out of a drawer. She glanced at Caius. He was staring at her, waiting for her response.

She sobered. 'Not that you need to have your cynicism boosted in any way, but no, they weren't in love.'

'So why were they together? She wasn't royal?'

Poppy shook her head. 'No, she wasn't. She's from America's Midwest. An aspiring actress and a model. My father saw her as some kind of a status symbol and I think my mother fancied herself as a Grace Kelly figure. My father was trying to make Valdere more glamorous.'

'I met a few women like that,' Caius said dryly.

'You were never tempted?' Poppy asked casually as she put the cutlery on the table and got some plates.

Caius was plating up the steaks and brought them over to the table. They looked and smelled delicious. He brought over sauce, salad and French fries. Wine for him, water for Poppy.

When he sat down Poppy said, 'This looks fantastic, thank you.'

He said, 'Your steak is well done. I checked to see what was safe.'

Poppy's fork stopped halfway to her mouth. 'Safe?'

He glanced down at her midriff. 'For the baby.'

Poppy gulped. 'Thanks, yes, it should be fine.' She was a little stunned that Caius had taken that into consideration. She took a bite of steak with sauce and it was unbelievably succulent and tasty. She groaned a little. 'This is so good, thank you. I was starving.'

Caius looked at her, eyes glinting. 'Me too.'

Poppy fought off a blush. Had they really just spent most of the day in bed together? The tenderness between her thighs was her answer.

When she'd swallowed a few more mouthfuls she said, 'You didn't answer me.'

Caius popped a French fry into his mouth and then said, 'About what?' But the innocence in his expression gave him away. She rolled her eyes.

'I asked if you weren't ever tempted to choose a wife—it's not as if you haven't had a lot of choice.'

She winced when she heard how that sounded. 'Sorry, I didn't mean it like that.'

'Don't worry, it takes a lot more than that to offend me.' He shook his head. 'And the answer is no. No one ever made me think about actually wanting a marriage outside what was required of me.'

Certainly not Poppy. As if she needed that reminder.

'But then,' he went on, 'I never really gave anyone a chance. I knew I didn't want to repeat my parents' mistakes and so I kept lovers at a distance. It was something I'd think about when I became king…but then a certain crown princess turned me down.'

He looked at her expressively and Poppy snorted a little. 'As if you expect me to believe I was the only princess you were in talks with.'

'Why did you turn me down?' Caius took a sip of wine, totally relaxed and looking unconcerned, but Poppy sensed a little tension.

'It was that conversation I heard you have with your advisors…when you spoke about having children and leaving me to live separately while you got on with your life…'

She went on, 'My father made me feel like a failure because I wasn't a son. I want more for my child…

children. I want them to feel wanted and cared for by two parents. Cherished. I don't think that's too much to ask for.'

'Your mother didn't make you feel loved?'

Poppy shrugged, avoiding Caius's eye now. 'She was humiliated by my father's rejection of her. I was a reminder of that. She moved on, married a rich businessman.'

She looked at Caius then, feeling a strong urge to make sure he knew she wasn't having a pity party. 'Look, I know our lives are very different from everyone else's and we have immense privilege, and I know there are no such things as fairy tales, but it's not a fairy tale to ask for a parent who cares.'

Caius said a little gruffly, 'Maybe we were just supremely unlucky with our parents.'

'You said your parents hated one another?'

He nodded. 'They argued all the time. My sister and I were classic examples of an heir and a spare—they had no interest in having more children. I tried to shield Cassie as much as I could from their never-ending drama but I'm not sure it worked. She's a people pleaser as a result, and hates conflict.'

'And you?'

He looked at her and said sardonically, 'Maybe that's the answer to your original question.'

Was he saying he was conflict avoidant? By avoiding relationships? She could understand that. She was rejection avoidant. But she was afraid she wasn't doing a very good job because sitting here talking to Caius properly for the first time was far too…easy. He wasn't at all what she'd expected.

'My sentiments haven't really changed, Poppy. I'm happy to take responsibility for my child and agree that five years is a decent amount of time to invest in giving them a secure beginning…and I'll be happy to work out an arrangement to be in their lives, but they'll be better off with you as a primary carer.'

'I didn't have good role models either, but I know I'll do everything in my power to nurture and love this child.' There was something very bleak about Caius's pronouncement.

'You'll be a good mother, Poppy. I would have been lucky to have you as my Queen of Sadat Sur Mer, but I think your instincts were right all along. I'm not the right partner for you in the long term.'

Poppy felt a rush of warmth that he thought she'd be a good mother. But then it fizzled when she registered the rest of what he'd said. He was agreeing with her. Ironic, now that they were married and having a child together.

But it was as if he'd written himself off a long time ago. After all, she'd heard him describe exactly what kind of a marriage he was willing to settle for. An arrangement where each spouse pretty much lived independently of the other, apart from duties.

Curious, she asked, 'Do you really think it's not possible to have something more? A real enduring committed partnership?' She wasn't going to expose herself by asking him if he believed in love when he clearly didn't and when the mere thought of being that vulnerable with another person made Poppy feel a little dizzy.

'Maybe that's the best one can hope for. And respect. The minute emotion comes into it, it turns into something toxic and volatile.' He looked at her. 'You're a romantic.'

Poppy sat up straight. 'Not at all.' But her betraying heart beat faster. 'I'm under no illusions about love, any more than you are.'

'It's not for me, but if it came along for you… I'd let you go.'

Something inside Poppy twisted. Would she let Caius go if he fell in love? For all of his talk, no man was an island and maybe when they were on the other side of their honeymoon and the baby was born and he still couldn't connect with the idea of a child, who was to say he might not finally meet someone who could crack him open and make him change his mind?

Unsettled by how that made her feel and not wanting to give Caius an inkling of what she was thinking, she gathered up the plates to bring over to the sink, but Caius put a hand on hers and immediately little shocks travelled up her arm.

'Leave them, I'll do it.' He took them from her and put them back down.

'You can wash too?' She sounded too sharp.

'I can stack a dishwasher.'

She felt gauche all of a sudden. She'd never navigated this situation. She'd never had a lover. Or a husband.

Hating the vulnerability she felt, she still had to ask, 'What are we doing here…? What is this?'

Caius drained his wine glass and put it down. He reached for Poppy's hand and linked their fingers. It felt shockingly intimate.

'We're doing what every other newly-wed couple on honeymoon are doing.'

Poppy rolled her eyes. 'Yes, but we're not every other newly-wed couple, are we?'

'Why worry about categorising it? Why not just enjoy it while it lasts?'

Poppy almost felt a rush of relief to be reminded of that and at the same time she felt a lurch of disappointment. She pulled her hand free. She was tempted to ask what would happen when it burned out but she didn't have to because she knew. Caius would go back to his life and pick up where he left off and leave her to get on with the running of her country.

He'd pay lip service to the marriage for five years and then he would divorce her and she would be a single parent. History repeating itself, except she vowed not to put her child through a whirling door of stepfathers.

The thought that something different could exist, something *real*, hovered in the air like a shimmering, delicate bubble for a moment and then the air was pierced by a sharp, strident sound, making Poppy jump.

Caius cursed and apologised, picking up his phone, which had been lying on the table. 'Sorry about this, it's Cass. I told her I needed to talk to her. I want to tell her about the baby before the press release goes out.'

Poppy waved a hand. 'Go ahead. I should probably check in with Stephen.'

Caius stood up and went out into the garden to take the call, his voice deep and warm. She felt jealous for a moment, of his sister for making him sound so warm. She was pathetic.

Poppy ignored his instruction to leave the plates and cleared up, still a little stunned that Caius had put together a meal.

She went back up through the chateau and into her private office, a pretty bright room during the day and cosy in the evening. She messaged Stephen to check all was OK and got back a voice note.

All is well here, everyone is still buoyant after the wedding. How are marital relations? Have you succumbed to his wicked charms again? I know I would—

There was the sound of Stephen's partner in the background. 'I am here, you know, in the room.'

Poppy smiled. Stephen went on to say that they were ready to push the button on the press release announcing the pregnancy. They knew that there would be no disguising the timing but at least this way the gossip would be less lurid if they were already married. Poppy took a second to think and then sent back a text message.

Go for it, send out the release x P

She threw the phone down and sighed. This was it, no going back. She'd made her bed and she would have to lie in it. Her skin prickled hotly at the thought of lying in Caius's bed again.

She longed to be the kind of woman who could feel

confident enough to be waiting for Caius in his bed, but the thought of him returning to his room and seeing her there and looking at her as if she was not welcome had her making her way back to her own bedroom.

She washed and got changed and into her night-clothes, the silk vest top and shorts. She caught sight of herself in the mirror in the bedroom and turned sideways. The bump was definitely growing. Those little flutters kept coming and going. She put her hands on it, unable to stop a small smile.

'That's what you were doing last night.'

Poppy looked up into the mirror to see Caius reflected behind her, standing in the adjoining door between her room and his.

'I did knock,' he said. 'But you're engrossed.'

Poppy felt breathless. 'It's hard not to be, it's such a strange sensation.'

'May I?'

Poppy nodded and watched as Caius came in and stood behind her. She looked up at him in the mirror. He was so tall. He came right up behind her and he pulled back her hair, so it lay behind her shoulders.

'You're beautiful,' he breathed. 'I don't know how I didn't see it.'

His blue gaze tracked down over Poppy's body. Her hands dropped away as he slid his hands around and put them on her belly. They were so big, they covered every inch of the burgeoning bump. Warm. Turning her blood molten.

'Can you feel the butterflies now?'

Yes. But not from the baby. She shook her head. 'It's stopped now.'

Their eyes met in the mirror. Blue and green. She looked very pale next to him. His hands moved upwards, pushing the silk vest up, until he cupped her breasts. Between Poppy's legs a pulse throbbed and she could feel the moist rush of desire.

'Look at yourself.'

She tore her gaze away from him to look and her legs nearly buckled. Her breasts overflowed Caius's palms. Fingers trapping her nipples. She looked so… bountiful, sensual.

He squeezed her flesh and she could feel his erection pressing against her. 'You still want me…'

He smiled in the mirror. 'Yes, Poppy, I still want you.' The smile faded. 'Right now, I can't imagine not wanting you.'

Caius couldn't believe he'd said those words out loud but they'd fallen out before he could stop them. He saw how Poppy's eyes widened. But he couldn't take them back because that was how he felt…right now. As if he couldn't imagine touching another woman again.

Not when his hands were full of her and he was so hard it hurt. He took his hands away from her momentarily and went to lift her top up and off. 'OK?'

She nodded, lifting her arms up. Now she wore only her shorts and they sat just under the small bump.

Caius came close again and massaged her breast with one hand while sliding the other one around, over the bump and then down, under the shorts, dislodging them.

'Spread your legs for me, Poppy.'

She did, and he explored down, through the springy curls around her sex to where she was hot and slick and so ready that he almost exploded there and then.

He watched her as he moved his fingers in and out, while squeezing her breast. Her breath came faster, and her skin flushed. Her eyes looked glazed and her mouth opened. She was biting her lip and her hips began to move, pressing her ass back against him, against his straining cock.

She brought her arm up and hooked it around Caius's neck, and her hips were undulating now as he thrust into her, deeper and deeper until she stopped and gave a keening cry as her inner muscles clamped down hard on his fingers.

Caius couldn't wait. He had to be in her right now or he would die. He removed his hand and pulled down her shorts and then turned her around as he undid his jeans and pushed them down, releasing his straining erection.

'I need to be in you, now, Poppy.'

She went over to the bed and got onto it and lay back, spreading her legs. He could see where she glistened from her orgasm. From his fingers. For a second Caius had to wonder if in fact she'd been some kind of sorceress all along and she'd bewitched him. She looked like an earth goddess with her curves and the one holding his child. It made him feel feral with a need to possess and also something else, a need to protect.

Somehow, he got naked and he came over her, guiding his aching, throbbing flesh to the centre of her body and sinking in slowly, mindful of her relative inexperience. But she raised her hips, forcing him to go deeper. He cursed. 'Poppy, I don't want to hurt you.' *Or the baby,* came into his mind. Of course, it was natural to care about the baby, he assured himself. He just hadn't ever expected sex with the mother of his child to feel so…intense.

He sank into her, to the hilt, and then pulled out, and back in, until every limb was shaking with the need to pound into her, slake his lust. She wrapped her legs around him. 'Take me, Caius, I'm not some delicate little flower.'

The tiny fraying piece of control he'd been clinging onto snapped. Caius pulled out and said roughly, 'Get on your knees, Poppy.'

She did, and she looked at him over her shoulder and he had no idea how he didn't spill there and then, but he managed to wait until he plunged into her tight sheath again, and he held her hips as he drove into her, over and over again until she was crying out and he reached under and found that little cluster of nerves and cells and pinched it. Poppy screamed as her body fell over the edge and the spasmodic contractions of her orgasm sent Caius flying so high he wasn't sure he'd ever come back down to earth again.

Eventually he did, collapsing back onto the bed and pulling Poppy into him. He felt the heavy slackness in her body. She was as spent as him. Normally he'd never countenance pulling a woman close after sex but he didn't usually feel as though he'd been through an earthquake.

And this was different. Poppy was his wife. The mother-to-be of his child. It was more or less sanctioned. It wasn't as if he had to be careful around her. They knew what this was. A temporary glitch in the mainframe.

And then he felt her breath feather over his skin as she asked sleepily, 'Is it always like this? Now I know why you liked it so much.'

Caius couldn't stop a half-grimace, half-smile at her innocent question. He knew it would be easy to tell her, *yes, it's always like this,* but he couldn't. He said, 'Truthfully? No. This is…rare.' Unprecedented. 'We have a very potent chemistry.'

She huffed a laugh against his chest. 'Just as well it'll burn out. I don't think I could survive if it was like this for ever.'

For ever. The word caused a twisting sensation inside Caius. There was no such thing. And yes, he was thankful this would burn out too, the sooner the better, because he was in danger of forgetting who he was, on this little island in the picture-postcard chateau with a queen who was confounding him at every turn.

The days after that night seemed to pass in a bit of a blur. A sex blur. It was as if Caius had awoken something inside Poppy, a part of herself that had been locked away, pushed down, denied, not given room to breathe…and now she couldn't stop breathing, taking massive gulps of air.

They were careful not to talk too much about anything more serious or personal than likes, dislikes, surface subjects, and as soon as it seemed respectable, they would let the staff go for the evening, Caius would cook, or Poppy would—from her own limited repertoire—and then they would go to bed. It was as if they'd made a tacit agreement to lean into indulging in this very traditional aspect of a very *un*traditional marriage.

This evening, they didn't even make it to dinner. Poppy's stomach gurgled and she turned her face into Caius's chest. It rumbled under her cheek as he laughed.

'Hungry?'

She lifted her head. 'Well, I am eating for two, you know.'

'Yes, you are.' Caius put his hand on her bump. It had grown—even in these few days—almost as if it were flowering under the attention. Poppy pushed the ridiculous notion aside. She knew this could be a time for a growth spurt.

'Are you going to find out the sex?'

Poppy tried not to love how much it felt to have Caius's hand on her, over where their child grew. She was afraid that actually she was in serious danger of forgetting the boundaries around this marriage. Sex was turning everything hazy and rose-tinted.

'I'm due my five-month scan in a couple of weeks. They can tell me—us—there. If you want to come.'

Caius shrugged minutely. 'I don't see why not. I do have to go back to New York for some meetings—maybe you could have it there?'

Poppy's heart kicked up a notch as she asked carefully, 'You want me to come?'

'Why not? I presume it'll be good for us to be seen together solidifying the fallacy that this is a fairytale royal union, after the honeymoon and news of the baby.'

Poppy hated how such cynicism tumbled from his mouth so easily. Especially when she was still tingling all over in the aftermath of making love.

She said, 'As it's just a scan, I'm sure my consultant here can set me up with someone there.'

'Great.'

Poppy made a move to get out of the bed so she could put on some clothes and make some food but Caius wrapped an arm around her and pulled her back down. He loomed over her and said with a devilish grin, 'I don't think your appetite is fully whetted, is it?'

'Caius,' Poppy groaned, but that groan turned to a moan of need as soon as his mouth settled over hers and his hands traced her curves and squeezed her waist, before exploring further, down between her legs where her body told her and him exactly where her real hunger lay.

Returning to Valdere a couple of days later, Poppy felt as if a layer of skin had been removed. She could see the throngs of people waiting for them to land and disembark from the short journey across the lake and they were cheering and waving flags.

Her heart constricted. She felt as if she were betraying them when, really, every marriage in her ancestry had been some form of an arrangement. Even though her father had been besotted with her mother, he'd wanted her because she was beautiful and glamorous and because he'd thought she'd help make Valdere seem more exciting, not because he'd really cared for her.

As the boat drew closer, Caius stood beside her and reached for her hand. Poppy looked up at him. He was wearing a suit, top button of his shirt was open. He looked casual but stylish. And sexy. Clotilde had come over earlier to help her get ready and she was wearing wide-legged trousers and a silk top in a matching colour, hair pulled back.

She no longer had to worry about hiding the bump and that was something of a relief because it really was growing.

When they disembarked, they were going to do a little walkabout. Caius let her go and they started on opposite sides of the street. It was a jolt to recognise that of course Caius didn't need to be given any kind of instruction. He knew what to do. He'd been doing it since childhood, like her.

She loved meeting the people and recognised quite a few faces, accepting flowers and presents. Everyone was so delighted that she was pregnant, there didn't seem to be any kind of hint of snide gossip. One little girl tugged on Poppy's trousers and she bent down and the girl said, 'Are you and the king like a real king and queen in a fairy tale?'

Poppy's heart constricted. She'd been that little girl once, wishing her parents could be really in love. The little girl was too young to understand and Poppy mentally crossed her fingers as she said, 'Of course we are.'

By the time she met Caius at the other end of the street leading away from the harbour her face was hurting from smiling. Caius took her hand and looked at her. 'OK?'

Poppy tried not to let it fool her—his easy civility. She nodded. 'Fine, feet are a bit sore.'

Caius made a gesture to the security and aides who'd met them and they were being ushered towards the car waiting for them. At the last moment someone from the crowd called out, *'Bisou!' Kiss!*

Caius stopped and pulled Poppy close, he bent his head and she lifted her face but before he kissed her he said, 'Just as well they can't see into my mind right now, or they'd be very shocked by their new king's lustful desires.'

Poppy's insides clenched. It had been mere hours since they'd been entwined in bed and she needed him again. Could it be pregnancy hormones? she wondered a little desperately as his mouth met hers and the crowd cheered.

Back at the palace they were served lunch on a private terrace. An aide approached as they were having tea and coffee to inform Caius that his office had now been fully set up, and that Stephen needed to see Poppy for a briefing.

When the aide had gone, Poppy said, 'I hope the office will be sufficient for your needs.'

'Do you want to talk about my needs?'

Poppy glanced around in case staff were hovering.

They seemed to be alone. It felt a lot more exposing to be back here at the palace, out of the bubble of the chateau. But not enough to care.

'Caius…'

'Yes?'

She looked at him and he was unrepentant. So arrogant in his confidence. But not arrogant in the way she'd first assumed. Her heart turned over at the cheeky but oh-so sexy look on his face, in his eyes. The fact that he'd been using that same expression for years to charm the pants off countless women made Poppy feel prickly. 'You're insatiable.'

He shook his head. 'I've never been this insatiable.'

And just like that Poppy's prickliness dissolved like snow on a hot stone. She was special. Was she? Right then she desperately wanted to believe she was special. One of the staff came back to clean the table. She saw the aide hovering nearby and said, 'Actually, I'm quite tired, would you mind telling Stephen that I'm going for a quick nap before my meeting?'

Caius stood up. 'I'll make sure you get to your room and that you're not disturbed.'

The aide scurried off to pass on the message.

When Poppy got to her rooms and Caius shut the door behind them and locked it, Poppy was breathless. She couldn't help giggling. She felt as if she were playing truant. This place had always been so serious, living under the dark cloud of her father's disappointment, and for the first time she felt light-hearted. *Oh boy.* She was in so much trouble already, because she knew it was second nature for Caius to be charming and seductive and mesmerising, but in this moment she didn't care. She wanted him too badly.

She wrapped her arms around Caius's neck. 'Take me to bed, Caius.'

He lifted her up into his arms. 'How can I disobey a direct order from my queen?'

For now, Poppy knew. While this intense absorption in each other lasted. She just hoped that when it ended, she would still be intact. At least she knew not to fall for him. Because for someone like her who'd survived the worst form of rejection, the rejection of a parent, she knew she wouldn't survive it again.

CHAPTER EIGHT

'NAP, MY ASS.'

Poppy looked up as Stephen came into her office a couple of hours later. Her body was still tingling.

She looked at him over her glasses. 'Is that any way to speak to your queen?'

He made a snorting sound and hitched his hip onto the corner of her desk. Poppy sat back.

'So, you *have* succumbed to the considerable charms of our new king consort. I can't say I blame you.'

Poppy fought off a blush and an illicit thrill to hear him described as *our king consort*. 'I don't know what you're talking about.'

Stephen waved a hand. 'Oh, please, we knew within twenty-four hours of your arrival on that island that you were indulging in very traditional marital relations.'

Poppy came forward and leaned her forehead on the desk, groaning softly. But then, she should have expected as much. It wasn't as if there were any such thing as secrets in a royal household.

She lifted her head again. 'And if I am?'

Stephen suddenly looked more serious. 'I heard him

on the phone that day too and he laid out pretty specifically how he expects the marriage to go…'

Poppy avoided Stephen's eye, pulling over a file. 'Yes, I don't need a reminder.' Her voice was too clipped.

Stephen stood up. 'Poppy…'

Reluctantly she looked at him and his eyes widened as if he'd seen something on her face. 'You're not… falling for him?'

The pit of Poppy's stomach seemed to open up. 'Don't be ridiculous.'

Stephen opened his mouth again but the ring of his phone sounded and he said, 'Saved by the bell,' as he answered the call and walked a little away from the desk.

Poppy stood up and walked over to the open French doors that opened out onto the terrace. She put her hands on the wall and gripped it tight, feeling a little dizzy.

It wasn't love, she assured herself—what she was feeling for Caius. He was a sexy, charismatic man and it would be impossible not to have a monumental crush on him but that was all it was.

Poppy was making up for lost time. She'd never had her rebellious moment. *What about Paris?* prompted a little voice. She ignored it.

She was also coming to terms with the fact that the Caius she'd spent time with over the last few days wasn't at all like the man she'd expected him to be. *He seduced you to pass the time on an island.* Even if he had denied that was the reason for wanting her, Poppy couldn't afford to forget who he really was, as Stephen had just said…

Stephen wrapped up his call and Poppy turned around ready to deny Stephen's suggestions but just as she opened her mouth, Caius appeared in the doorway of her office, saying apropos of nothing, 'You have horses.'

'Um, yes,' said Poppy, a little shocked to see him there, her gaze tracking avidly over his powerful physique in dark trousers and a blue shirt that made his eyes pop even more. His hair was still damp from the shower he'd insisted they take together after making love. Her insides clenched. She struggled to focus. 'We've always had horses here. We're famous for our riding trails that go up into the mountains.'

'Is it safe for you to horse ride when pregnant?'

Poppy shrugged. 'I don't see why not. It's not as if we'd be galloping.'

She looked at Stephen, who put out a hand, saying, 'I can double-check with the doctor, but why don't you go to the stables in the meantime and I'll let you know?'

Poppy looked at Caius and he held out his hand. As if pulled by a stronger force she went and put her hand in his and let him lead her out of her office, studiously avoiding looking at her friend and advisor. She could feel his smirk.

An hour later, Caius was changed into jeans and a T-shirt and on a horse on a narrow winding uphill trail. Poppy was ahead of him on her own horse, similarly dressed, hair pulled back into a low ponytail, wearing a hard hat. Her hair was a vivid splash of red against the white of her polo shirt.

She moved as one with the horse with graceful command. An innate horsewoman.

Cauis had always loved horses and had played polo over the years but he'd never really had time to ride recreationally. When the trail widened out a bit, he came alongside Poppy and she looked at him and smiled. 'You look relaxed.'

Caius realised he was relaxed. More relaxed than he could remember feeling in a long time. And he couldn't discount the pleasurable after-effects of lovemaking lingering in his blood.

'You have horses in Sadat?' Poppy asked.

He shook his head. 'Not now. We did, when I was young, but my mother had a fall and my father got rid of the horses and built over the stables.'

'Oh no… I can understand why maybe, but to take such a drastic step?'

'He didn't do it out of any romantic notion for his wife's safety, he did it because she was having an affair with one of the groomsmen.'

'Oh.'

'Yes, *oh*,' echoed Caius.

After a moment Poppy asked, 'Was he your father? Or do you even know who he is?'

Caius's insides clenched tight. Poppy said, 'Forget I asked, it's none of my business.'

Caius shook his head. 'It's fine. And it is your business, we're having a child together. The truth is that I don't know. Both my parents had died before I knew about my birth. I can probably do some detective work to find out, but as yet no one has crawled out of the woodwork, which is surprising given the very public nature of the way the news was announced.'

'How did it come out?'

'There's a small contingent of anti-monarchists in Sadat and they were determined to disrupt my rule. Somehow they were able to hack into the royal family medical records and discovered I have a rare blood type, different from the rest of the family. They did more digging and found that my father's DNA and mine didn't match.'

Poppy asked, 'How long beforehand did you know? Before it became public knowledge?'

'Hours. We got a call from the editor of the local tabloid letting us know what they had and that they were publishing as it was in the public interest.'

Poppy winced. 'That was rough.'

Caius let out a laugh. 'One way of describing it.' He could remember all too well the way his insides had seemed to turn to liquid. And the awful sense of exposure—as if the reason why he'd always felt so redundant was now laid bare for all to see and he had nothing to hide behind any more.

'Maybe your biological father doesn't even know, himself,' Poppy pointed out. Caius made a dismissive sound.

'Do you want to know who your father is?'

Caius shrugged but he was sure his nonchalance didn't fool Poppy. He said, 'I can't say I'd hold out much hope for a happy reunion and my experience of fathers so far leaves much to be desired. Maybe I'm better off not knowing.'

'You could have family, brothers and sisters.'

He looked at Poppy. 'I have a sister.' And he'd given her enough of a burden to carry without concerning himself with other potential siblings.

Fair enough. Poppy got the hint, subject closed. She couldn't exactly argue with his view on fathers. She felt something poignant grip her to imagine that Caius might actually have the experience of bonding with his child in a way that could restore his faith in what a parent could be.

And this coming from her, who'd had not much better of an experience than him! But still…she had somehow managed to hold onto a sense of hope for something better.

At that moment a bird flew out from a bush nearby, startling the horses, who skittered. Caius immediately caught Poppy's reins and held onto her horse. He looked at her. 'Are you OK?'

'I'm fine, it's fine. The horses are used to wildlife in the woods.'

Neverthless, Caius got off his horse and led it and Poppy's horse onwards.

She said, 'Caius, really, don't worry.' But her heart was hammering a little bit at the lightning-fast way Caius had intercepted.

When they got to a small mountain lake, Poppy got off her horse and they tied them off to trees nearby where they could access water and be in the shade.

They sat down on a picnic blanket and Caius took out the water and snacks they'd been given to bring. Poppy said, 'I'm meant to be taking a meeting with Stephen.'

Caius said, 'And I'm meant to be having a conference call with my team in New York. But you can count on me for distraction and deflection, I'm an expert.'

'Distraction from what?' Poppy asked. But then she remembered something he'd said that had struck her days ago, but it had got pushed aside in the heat of their mutual combustion, and before he could answer she added, 'You said something back on the island about courting the media partly to get your parents' attention. What else were you using them for, if not to distract?'

Caius looked at her. 'Do you have some kind of supersonic memory?'

She smiled sweetly. 'No, I'm just very intelligent and I listen.'

Caius looked visibly reluctant to answer but Poppy stayed silent, waiting. He sighed volubly. 'I think I was always conscious of the fact that I'd been born for no other reason than to continue a line. I never felt like I deserved to be a king. Maybe it was because I picked up on my father's suspicions…who knows? I was conscious of others looking at me and wondering what my purpose was. And I didn't want Cassie to be brought into their crosshairs, so I distracted them.'

That struck Poppy as being incredibly poignant. She could relate to Caius's feeling of being an outsider, albeit for different reasons. She knew he wouldn't welcome her sympathy though.

He put a grape in his mouth as he handed her the bunch. She took a grape too and its sweetness burst in her mouth. She'd noticed that lots of things were more heightened since she'd become pregnant.

She hoped that could explain her fascination with Caius.

He said, 'I was born specifically to fulfil a role and I failed.'

Poppy rolled her eyes. 'You didn't fail. Your parents failed. You didn't ask to be born illegitimate, into a royal family.'

'Nevertheless, I had a duty and now my sister has to bear that burden.'

Poppy could hear the self-censure in his voice. For the first time she had a full appreciation of how much Caius had blamed himself for something that had been completely out of his control.

'Your parents had a duty to you, to support and guide and protect.'

Caius made a face. 'My father suspected I wasn't his, and my mother most likely knew. So between her guilt and his suspicion and their fights, there was no time for anything else. In any case, they had no ability or desire to care about anyone else but themselves.'

Poppy knew what that looked like. Lightly she said, 'It looks like your sister has good support in her fiancé. They seem to be genuinely in love.'

'Ares was my best friend. I sent him to protect Cassie and he ended up seducing her.'

Poppy laughed. 'From the little I saw of your sister,

I can imagine she had some say in the matter and I'm sure Ares is still your best friend.'

'Maybe, when I can excise the images of them together out of my head.'

Poppy was touched by Caius's obvious affection for his sister and friend. He could love. It made something dangerous inside her bloom.

He reached for her and pulled her down with him so she lay in sprawl over him.

'I think you're a fraud, Caius Mansur,' she said.

His expression shuttered. 'What do you mean?'

'I mean, I think there's a lot more to you than you want people to think.'

He shook his head. 'That's just it, there really isn't. This is it.'

But there was more to him. Poppy was seeing that now. He felt deeply, even if he wouldn't admit it.

But before she could probe or see any further, Caius caught a lock of hair in his fingers and tugged her head down. Her mouth hovered over his for an infinitesimal moment as if she could pretend she was capable of resisting his pull, but he lifted his head, and their mouths touched and any hope of resistance was gone.

He moved them so that she was on her back and he was on his side. The kiss became hungry and desperate in seconds and Caius reached for her jeans, snapping them open.

T-shirts were pulled off, Poppy had one leg in her jeans, the other free, Caius's jeans were pulled down around his ankles and when he joined their bodies, Poppy bit into his shoulder to stop herself from crying out even though they were surrounded by nothing but snow-capped mountains and the lake and grazing horses.

It was fast and messy and sweaty and glorious, under the shade of the trees. Afterwards, as their skin cooled and heartbeats returned to normal, Poppy was tempted to tell Caius he couldn't distract and deflect for ever, but she realised that that was exactly what he'd just done to her.

Two weeks later, Manhattan

It felt jarring to be back in a big city after the last few weeks in Valdere, in the clear, high mountain air, with the big endless sky. Now it was hard to even see much sky with all the soaring skyscrapers.

Or maybe, it was that Poppy felt exposed. Vulnerable. And it wasn't pregnancy hormones. It was Caius.

They were here because Caius had meetings and Poppy had agreed to come. She was on the board of several charitable organisations so there was always something to do if she was in New York, and, as Caius had pointed out, it would be good to appear in public, solidifying the illusion of their marriage.

The only problem with that was the fact that it didn't feel like so much of an illusion to Poppy. It felt far more disturbingly ambiguous and hard to define.

The last two weeks had passed as if in a kind of dream, a dream she'd never dared hope might exist, because she'd certainly never seen it between her father and any of his wives, including her mother. She and Caius had settled into a rhythm. They would spend the nights together in his room or hers. They had separate rooms but adjoining suites, much like the chateau on the island.

Mornings were spent working in their respective offices and then they'd go horse riding in the afternoons. Caius looked ten years younger on the back of a horse, his face relaxed, body at ease, moving as one with the horse. They'd explored a lot of trails and Poppy had taken him to some of her favourite private spots, revealing that she'd escape there to avoid her father's ever-present disappointment or the inevitable arguments between him and his latest wife when no children materialised.

One day she'd asked, 'You're really not missing the social whirl?' She'd hated herself for asking, fearing it exposed her insecurity.

He'd glanced at her, mouth tipping up slightly. 'Remember what I said about twenty per cent?'

Poppy had pointed out, 'Twenty per cent of *your* social activity was still probably more than most see in a lifetime.'

He'd laughed and it had made Poppy feel as if she'd won something, because it was a genuine laugh.

He'd said after a while, 'I'd started to pull back in preparation for becoming king. I was making sure my business was set up under new management while I would be in Sadat more often. Not that the media would have you believe it. They just rehashed old photos and video footage and made it look like I was out every night.'

Poppy had teased, ‘So you weren’t really there that night in Paris? It was a mirage?’

He’d looked at her and then down at her bump and back up to catch her face flaming. ‘No, that was very real. The most real thing that had happened to me in a long time.’

They’d been riding and the trail had narrowed so Caius had gone ahead—since that first day he’d been mindful of the horses getting spooked—and Poppy had looked at his broad back and tried to figure out exactly what he’d meant by that statement. Had he meant it negatively? Or positively? It had been impossible to know from his tone of voice.

But, of course, within minutes he’d been employing one of his expert methods of distraction. They didn’t even have to be expert—all he had to do was look at her in a certain way and she forgot her name.

The SUV was pulling to a stop outside a tall, elegant apartment building on the edge of Central Park. She’d been here before, the day she’d come to tell Caius about the pregnancy and he’d brought her here from his office.

He got out of the car and came around to her side and opened the door, holding out his hand. Poppy took it, and a little electric current ran up her arm, making her fingers tighten reflexively on Caius’s. They shared a look for a moment and Poppy could swear she saw something almost like bewilderment in Caius’s eyes. As if to say, *How can I still want her?*

But then he was leading her into the building and up the elevator to the penthouse apartment. It was as impressive as she remembered, huge picture windows looking over the park and doors opening out onto a generous terrace that was on different levels.

'I didn't show you around the last time,' Caius mentioned dryly.

'Um, no,' Poppy said. No, the last time had been fraught to say the least.

'Let me remedy that now.' Caius still had Poppy's hand in his and she dropped her bag as he led her from the impressive reception area with its elegant couches, coffee tables and chairs to the sleek kitchen with its own little eating area. Beside that was a formal dining room that could seat a football team.

There was a media room with a home cinema, a gym with a lap pool and a spacious home office. Caius gestured. 'Feel free to use this as your office too.'

Then upstairs there were numerous bedrooms and en suites. The master suite took up an entire corner with windows taking in an almost three-hundred-and-sixty-degree view of Manhattan.

Poppy shook her head. 'This is stunning, Caius.' Even for someone like her, who had grown up around a certain level of wealth and luxury.

'It's the first property I bought with my own money.'

She looked at him and sensed his pride and assessed, 'It's important to you, isn't it? To have done this on your own?'

He nodded a little. 'Maybe because I always sensed that I was a cuckoo in the nest, I had an instinctive need to prove myself.'

Before Poppy could respond to that a woman dressed

in smart black trousers and a shirt knocked on an adjoining door that led into a vast dressing room and said, ‘Your things are unpacked. Will you be dining in this evening?’

Caius looked at Poppy and raised a brow in question. Poppy realised she felt a bit weary after the journey and because they weren’t exactly getting much sleep at night. She said, ‘I’m a little tired and the twenty-week scan is early tomorrow. I might stay in, but you should go out if you like?’

Poppy figured Caius must be chomping at the bit to get back to his social scene, no matter what he’d said about ‘twenty per cent’. But he said to the woman, ‘We’ll both be in for the evening, if you can let chef know, please.’

‘Certainly.’ The woman left.

Poppy took her hand from Caius’s. For some reason she felt a little on edge. As if Caius choosing to stay in was more unsettling than if he’d gone out. ‘Don’t feel like you have to babysit me, Caius. If you want to go out, it’s no problem, really.’

‘And equally, it’s no problem to stay in. Unless you’d prefer to be alone?’

This was said lightly but Poppy could sense an undertone of something, something that almost made her feel a little guilty for suggesting she might not want to spend the evening with Caius. She shook her head. ‘No, of course not… I just…’

‘You just expect me to want to go clubbing at the first opportunity.’

‘I…maybe,’ Poppy admitted, feeling a little foolish now. She had to concede that it had been weeks, months, since Caius had graced a tabloid with his antics. Was she trying to push him back to some kind of safe distance because the truth was that she'd never expected him to become embedded—literally—in her life so easily?

Because she'd never expected to want to spend time with him? *Because she'd never expected to need him.*

'In fact…' Caius reached for her now, hands on her thickening waist, and tugged her towards him '…I feel a little tired too, maybe we should both take a nap before dinner.'

Poppy felt like groaning at the inevitable way her body lit up for Caius, like an instrument, vibrating in his presence. But then his mouth was on hers and the spectacular backdrop of Manhattan and everything else—all the concerns in her head—fell away as she allowed Caius to transport them both away from thinking about anything.

The following morning the trip to the medical clinic was short. Poppy had felt shy since seeing Caius at breakfast on the terrace outside the kitchen. Making love yesterday afternoon into evening…there'd been an edge of desperation to it, almost as if both of them were freaked out that this insatiable desire wasn't waning. It was getting stronger.

'OK?'

Poppy glanced at Caius in the back of the SUV and then couldn't look away. He was simply gorgeous. In a white shirt and dark trousers. Hair thick and just this side of acceptable messy. Beard short and hugging his hard jaw. Mouth sculpted and—

She looked away before he realised she was staring at him like a groupie, and admitted, 'Just a bit apprehensive, I guess. I haven't had a scan since the very first one.' Truth be told, Caius was an all too effective distraction from any concerns she might have about the pregnancy.

He took her hand and she looked at him. He said, 'I'm sure it'll be fine.'

Poppy's insides swooped dangerously. Caius Mansur de Roche, one of the world's most notorious playboys, holding her hand and reassuring her? Not to mention marrying her to make their unborn child legitimate and then endearing himself to the people of Valdere by being charming and respectful?

Everyone seemed to have formed a crush on their new king consort, from the grooms at the stable who'd watched, slack-jawed, as Caius had insisted on washing his and Poppy's horses and mucking out the stables, to the students at Valdere's university who'd asked him to come in and talk about his career in finance.

Not to mention the people in the smaller villages in the mountains who couldn't recall the last time they'd had a visit from a king. Poppy's father certainly hadn't been bothered visiting beyond Valdere City, so she'd made it a priority to do regular visits after his death, but her novelty factor had faded considerably next to Caius, when he'd accompanied her on the latest trip.

Out of the bubble of the wedding and honeymoon and here against the backdrop of New York, it was even more stark just how surprising Caius was. And how much Poppy feared she was in danger of forgetting to protect herself.

She pulled her hand free. 'I'm sure you're right.'

He frowned at her minutely but then the driver was saying, 'We're here, Your Highnesses.'

Within minutes they were in a room in the clinic with the efficient consultant and Poppy was on a bed with her top pulled up to expose her expanding belly. The consultant had put gel on her belly and the lights were turned down so they could see the monitor better.

'Ready?'

Poppy nodded. Caius said, 'Yes, thank you.'

The doctor pressed the wand into Poppy's belly and moved it around. It took a minute but then the rapid sound of the baby's heartbeat filled the room and an unmistakable grainy image of a foetus came onto the screen. A hand lifted as if it was waving and the doctor said with a smile, 'The baby is waving at you.'

And then, 'All looks healthy and exactly as it should be. Do you want to know the sex?'

Poppy was still reeling to see the baby and hear that all was well. She looked up at Caius, who was staring at the screen with wide eyes and—it was hard to know in this dim light, but it looked as if he'd gone pale. 'Caius?'

He dragged his gaze to hers. She said, 'Do we want to know the sex?'

'You decide.'

Poppy realised that they really had no choice, not for a significant birth like this. 'OK, yes, please.'

The doctor looked at them both and said, 'Well, then, I'm delighted to let you know you're having a little girl.'

Poppy let out an involuntary sound of happiness, putting her hand to her mouth. Caius said hoarsly, 'A girl?'

The doctor nodded. 'Yes. Congratulations.' She wiped the gel off Poppy's belly and turned the lights back on. She said, 'I'll leave you to take it in. I'll be outside when you're ready.'

She left the room and Poppy pulled her top down. Caius still looked a little shell-shocked. She sat up and swung her legs over the side of the bed. 'Caius?'

He looked at her, dazed. Something occurred to her and she felt a little sick. Why hadn't she thought of it before? Her hands tightened on the edge of the bed. 'You're disappointed it's a girl.'

He looked at her, unseeing for a moment and then, with comprehension dawning, 'What?'

Poppy stood up. 'You wanted a boy?' She'd been so blind, she'd never even considered this.

Caius's eyes narrowed on her as if hearing her thoughts. 'No, Poppy. *No.* I am not your father. I don't share his prejudice about gender. It just…wasn't what I was expecting.'

She felt vulnerable. 'Do you mean it? You don't mind? I'm changing the law in Valdere so a girl can rule if she's the firstborn.'

She wanted him to reach for her, touch her, but he stayed back. He shook his head. 'Of course I don't mind. All that matters is that they're healthy and happy.'

Words she'd not expected to hear coming out of Caius's mouth. Now she felt wrong-footed. As if she'd disappointed him with her misjudgement.

They left the room and the doctor reassured them again that all was well and told them to let her know if they needed anything else.

Caius was silent on the journey back to the apartment. When the car pulled up outside the building he said, 'I'm going to go into the office. I'm not sure how late I'll be.'

Poppy nodded. 'OK.' And then she stopped. 'Caius, I'm sorry that I assumed you wouldn't want a girl. It wasn't fair.'

'No, but it's understandable after your experiences.'

She got out of the car and then watched as it left again, merging into the Manhattan traffic heading downtown. She hated to admit she felt she needed more reassurance. But Caius had gone somewhere else in his head, somewhere she had no access to.

It reminded her of the impenetrable wall around her father and the way he'd never give an inkling as to what he was thinking because he didn't think Poppy's opinion was required or valid.

Poppy hated that Caius's response was triggering her. As he'd said, he wasn't her father. No. But he obviously also had the ability to make her feel shut out. And she'd let that happen because she'd lowered her guard and let him under her skin.

Poppy told herself she was glad now that he hadn't witnessed this little moment of neediness. Maybe this seismic experience of seeing the baby made flesh—a little girl—and being back in his old milieu of a glamorous metropolis would remind Caius of what he'd given up and that Poppy wasn't as tempting as she'd been in Valdere.

And maybe, that would be for the best.

CHAPTER NINE

MUCH LATER THAT EVENING, Caius returned to a quiet and darkened apartment. A few low lights were on. No sign of Poppy. He'd sent her a message earlier to let her know not to wait up.

He slipped off his jacket and went to stand at one of the windows that displayed only the darkness of the park—a ring of lights in buildings around it.

He could still see Poppy's worried expression on her face as he'd left earlier. She knew he'd been freaked. *She'd believed that he wouldn't want a girl.* That had hit him like a punch to the gut, that she would put him in the same category as her toxic father.

And yet he got it. He understood. But for a second, he'd been hurt. And the realisation that she had the power to hurt him was more shocking than the scan experience and hearing that rapid heartbeat of his daughter. Or that image of her curled in the womb, utterly vulnerable and dependent.

Just looking at his daughter on that monitor earlier had roused a feeling like a balloon expanding in his chest, so much so that he could hardly breathe.

Until today the baby had been this abstract concept, but not any more. She was there. She existed. She would exist. He'd found himself wondering if she would have Poppy's distinctive hair. Maybe his eyes?

He'd felt an overwhelming sense of responsibility and fear, which he'd felt only once before when he'd realised that his parents weren't capable of caring for him or his sister, and that he was the only one his sister could count on, and ultimately he'd let her down. Would he inevitably do it again to his own daughter? In spite of his best efforts?

He'd tried to be there for Cassie—no matter what Caius was doing or where he was in the world, he'd never let himself get so sidelined that he couldn't be available to go to her if she needed him. She was the only one who had seen through the carefully cultivated bon viveur facade. She knew what lay beneath—the fear of his emotions getting the better of him. Because they'd both seen what emotions gone out of control looked like—toxic chaos. Screaming matches. A royal house reduced to a shell of itself. All of your naked vulnerabilities laid bare for everyone to see.

Even now, the thought of such exposure made Caius cringe inwardly. No one would ever have that power over him, he assured himself. And yet, after today, the assertion rang a little hollow. Because already the thought of a daughter was triggering all sorts of deeply buried emotions. How could a daughter not see through him?

Like her mother? asked a little voice. As much as he didn't want to admit it, Poppy knew he was hiding behind a construct—he'd spilled his guts to her! The foundations upon which Caius had conducted his life for so long felt increasingly shaky.

It hit him then, the memory of how empty he'd felt at that party in Paris, in spite of being crowned king. And how, since the subsequent encounter with Poppy, he hadn't felt that same level of emptiness. Not even during the scandal of his parentage and abdication.

He'd felt many other things—frustration, anger, shame, guilt. But not that awful clawing feeling of, *is this it?* And since Poppy had appeared back in his life, turning it upside down, the last thing he'd been feeling was empty or directionless.

Obeying an instinct stronger than the one he had to cut and run, Caius made his way through the apartment and up to the bedroom. Poppy was in his bed. Something about that was immensely satisfying. He told himself it was just because he wanted her and it was more convenient having her in his bed than not.

He stripped off his clothes and got into the bed. Poppy was on her side. She turned towards him sleepily. 'Caius?'

Caius pushed down the maelstrom inside him. 'Well, I would hope so, or you'd be in trouble.'

She opened her eyes fully and they widened when she took in that he was naked. She said, 'It's late.'

'I stayed at the office, working. And… I needed a moment, after that scan.' Understatement of the century.

Poppy reached up and touched his face, tracing his jaw. Caius felt something threaten to erupt inside him.

But he ruthlessly pushed it down. He put his hand over Poppy's, interlacing their fingers.

She said, 'Do you want to talk about it?'

'No,' Caius said quickly. Too quickly.

Poppy huffed a little laugh and reached for him with her other arm, tugging him down so that all he could feel were her abundant curves and one in particular that cradled his child.

He kissed Poppy deeply. When he pulled back they were both breathing heavier and she said, 'You still want me.'

Caius frowned. Was she mocking him? He wanted her so much he ached all over. 'Yes,' he said, sounding harsh. 'Of course I still want you.'

He kissed her again, pulling away the sheet and helping her out of her nightclothes until she was gloriously naked and arching against him, making his blood boil over with lust.

This wouldn't last, it couldn't. And if he felt ruthless now for seeking out the physical to avoid thinking about everything else…well, wasn't that his modus operandi? So nothing had changed at all really. Nothing.

The following evening a team of stylists and make-up and hair people were putting finishing touches to Poppy's outfit. They were going to a charity function, part of the PR drive to be seen in public—the first official international public outing for the happy royal couple.

Poppy was wearing a black strapless dress with a structured bodice that dipped between her breasts and fell in long loose folds to the floor. It disguised but didn't totally hide her bump.

Her hair was down and she wore a stunning emerald and diamond necklace that Caius had had delivered from one of the big jewellery houses. Apart from that and her wedding rings, Poppy was unadorned.

Caius was waiting for her in the reception area, wearing a tuxedo with a white jacket and black bow tie. The white made him look even darker. He took her breath away and she had to hold onto the bannister to stop tripping over her own feet.

It was only when she was standing in front of him that she saw how his blue eyes were looking her up and down, lingering on her midriff and then up, to where her fuller than normal breasts were showcased by the bodice of the dress. She felt beautiful under Caius's avid gaze. And she knew she shouldn't get used to it, but it would take the strength of someone far stronger than her to resist the lure to glory in it. For so long she'd felt unseen and unwanted.

'You are stunning, Poppy.'

'Thank you, you look good too.'

His mouth quirked. 'Just good?'

Poppy rolled her eyes as her face got hot. 'As if you don't know how good you look.'

He came close and cupped her face in his hand. She wanted to turn her face into it and purr like a cat.

Caius said, 'You look at me in a way no one has looked at me before. Like you don't want anything from me.'

Poppy's heart skipped a beat. 'Is that a good thing?' Because she did want him, with a ceaseless craving.

He nodded. 'Yes. I like it.' He dropped his hand and caught hers, leading her out of the apartment.

The driver was waiting outside and the journey to one of Manhattan's oldest buildings didn't take long. There was a red carpet leading up the steps and into the building, lanterns along the way, illuminating the guests as they made their way in.

As soon as the media recognised Caius and Poppy they went wild. *King Caius! Queen Poppy! Over here, please, look this way!* The clamour was almost overwhelming. Poppy was more used to the media not recognising her because she'd always stayed below the radar—so this was intense. But Caius had a strong arm around her and she unashamedly relished the sense of protection.

'Caius! We've missed you! Will you be at the polo match?'

Poppy felt Caius tense beside her and then he said with a forced joviality, 'I can't say I've missed you too.'

There was laughter and then a more snide and pointed question. 'They say leopards never change their spots—are you really a reformed man, King Caius?'

Caius stopped again and his hand tightened on Poppy's but she didn't say anything. His jaw looked hard enough to crack. Then he faced the wall of paparazzi and pulled Poppy even closer, saying, 'How could I not be reformed when I have this beautiful woman as my wife?' He looked down at her and Poppy had only an inkling of what was coming when Caius bent his head and pressed a hard kiss to her mouth.

Then it was over and he was leading her into the venue, a museum that had been transformed into a magical setting featuring thousands of candles and the outdoors seemingly transplanted indoors with plants and trees and vines covering almost every surface.

Her mouth still tingled after that kiss. That hadn't been a kiss. She'd felt the pent-up emotion that had nothing to do with her. She pulled her hand away and Caius looked at her. 'Are you OK? Did I hurt you?'

Poppy shook her head quickly, terrified he'd see shades of the neediness and hurt she'd felt yesterday after the scan. Caius had been caught up somewhere in his past just now, where she couldn't reach. Again. Another reminder of letting him in too deep. She'd been so pathetically relieved last night when she'd woken and found him in bed. Wanting her. Now she wanted to kiss *him* hard, to punish him for making her want him. Need him.

'No, but don't use me like that again to make a point.'

Caius cursed, and faced her. 'I'm sorry. I just…hate them. They're parasites but I let them feed off me for a long time and so I was frustrated because I hate myself for it too, for creating that monster. And now I've brought you onto their radar. They're insatiable.'

Poppy's hurt and anger diminished at his honesty and a part of her now was glad she had been there for him in the moment. That he had allowed her to feel that emotion even if it had been directed at himself.

'I'm responsible for bringing myself onto their radar too. I can handle it, Caius. What was the polo match they mentioned?'

'It's an annual match for charity. I usually play with the European team against the South Americans.'

'And you're not?'

'I hadn't even thought of it. It's the week after next.'

'I've never been to a polo match.'

Caius raised a brow. 'I can let them know I'm available to play if you want to go?'

Poppy smiled at Caius, glad to see that he'd visibly relaxed since the barrage outside. 'That sounds like fun.'

Caius watched Poppy deep in conversation with a diplomat's wife. She was fascinating to observe. She invested her whole self in whoever she was talking to. Not looking over people's shoulders like so many in this kind of situation, looking for the next more important person to appear.

And, as a result of her genuine interest and attention, people walked away from her smiling, glowing.

She was also very easy to look at in that dress that seemed to defy gravity, showcasing her generous breasts and acres of pale skin. Her red hair stood out in the crowd and Caius liked that he could find her easily. She'd gone to the bathroom earlier and he'd found himself unable to focus properly until he'd seen that distinctive red head reappearing on the other side of the room.

When she'd appeared to be getting stopped by every

single person en route back to where he'd been, he'd simply cut a swathe through the crowd to get to her. She'd met his eye just before he'd reached her and sent a silent message of *get me out of here, please*, and Caius had duly obliged, taking her hand and telling her rapt audience apologetically that he had to introduce her to someone.

He had to admit he was still a little off-centre after the interaction with the paparazzi, and then with Poppy. That kiss had been born out of frustration, yes, but there had also been a lot more going on. He'd felt a need to counteract that snide remark insinuating that he couldn't change.

Insinuating that maybe Poppy wasn't enough. Caius had felt anger rise, and suddenly he'd been kissing her, an instinctive reaction.

But now he could see that he would never have turned to another woman and had that response. He would have smiled and employed the charm that had become his stock-in-trade response.

But he couldn't do that around Poppy because he could no more be superficial with her than he could keep pretending that she hadn't got to him deeper than anyone else. Like the way she was all the way embedded deeper in his life than anyone else ever had been.

And it wasn't just because of the pregnancy. She wouldn't *be* pregnant if their connection hadn't been so deep and visceral the first night they'd met.

They'd connected emotionally. *No.* The rejection of that assertion was immediate. They were having a baby. They were married. He wanted her. He felt protective of her, naturally. That was all.

The vast space was emptying out. Caius was surprised. He was used to coming to events like this, tolerating it for as long as possible, which wasn't usually very long, and then seeking out the next event to try and keep his interest alive.

But that no longer appealed. What did appeal was the thought of getting back to the apartment with Poppy and forgetting about that disturbing interlude with the paparazzi and ridiculous thoughts of how he couldn't recall what it felt like to be in a situation like this with anyone else and undoing that dress so that he could fill his hands with her—

'Can we go dancing?'

Caius blinked and focused on Poppy, who was looking up at him. She said, 'Celeste said there's a new place opening tonight.'

'Celeste?'

'The French ambassador's assistant.'

The thought of going to a nightclub opening filled Caius with a sense of ennui. He opened his mouth to say no but then thought of something. 'Are you suggesting this because you think it's what I want?'

'I haven't been out dancing since I was in university and those places were dives. I've never been to a proper club.'

'You're pregnant!' Caius was aware he sounded like someone twice his age. An indignant father.

Poppy rolled her eyes. 'I'm not handicapped, Caius. The baby will probably love the music.'

She looked so young in that moment, face open and excited, eyes shining. Caius felt jaded. Like the buzz kill. And yet her infectious enthusiasm lit something inside. A need to indulge. Feeling sure she'd hate it once they got there, he shrugged and said, 'OK, fine, let's go.'

But Poppy didn't hate it. She loved it. Even with a sparkling water instead of sparkling wine. Even wearing an evening gown when everyone else was more appropriately attired. She loved the glamour of it, the dance floor with its retro lit-up squares and the disco balls. The private booths and the funky mix of house and pop music.

She was swaying to the beat, looking at the crowd, drinking it all in. She could feel the baby kicking and turned to Caius where he was sitting in the booth looking at her. She came over to him, hands on her belly, and said over the pounding base, 'The baby is dancing too!'

He pulled her down onto his lap and put his hands on her belly, Poppy moved them to where she'd felt the kicks and the baby kicked again under Caius's hand. She saw his eyes widen and cheeks flush. She felt a surge of emotion and had to blink it back.

The moment felt incredibly intimate even though Poppy knew the backdrop was the antithesis of intimate. It was public. Loud. Frantic. She caught Caius's hand and stood up. 'Dance with me?'

But Caius shook his head. 'I don't dance in places like this, Poppy.'

She let his hand go and stuck her tongue out, before saying, 'I don't care if it's not cool, I'm dancing.'

Before Caius could stop her, she'd gone beyond the VIP cordon and down the stairs and onto the dance floor. He stood up and went to the rail, putting his hands on it, searching for Poppy's distinctive hair in the crowd and then he found her, in the middle, holding her dress up with one hand, and moving to the beat in a way that was both endearingly offbeat and seriously sexy.

She couldn't dance. That much was obvious. But she didn't care and wasn't attracting sniggers, quite the opposite. She was attracting attention. Mostly from men, eyeing up her curves. Poppy was oblivious, dancing in her own little world, smiling to herself. She seemed younger, carefree.

Something surged within Caius. He only realised it was jealousy when he was halfway across the dance floor to insert himself between her and a growing rapt audience.

She looked up at him and smiled and he couldn't help smiling back because his hands were full of her and the jealous beast inside him could breathe again. They moved together and Caius forgot about everyone else as they moved to a different beat.

She suddenly reached up and pressed a kiss to his mouth, hard, and then pulled back. Caius asked, 'What was that for?'

Poppy looked pleased with herself. 'Earlier. A kiss for a kiss. Now we're quits.'

But they weren't quits at all, because Caius suddenly

realised he'd wanted to distract himself from thinking about earlier revelations by losing himself in Poppy but he was here, enjoying himself far too much, when these places had never really held much of an appeal for him, after his teenage years.

Another unwelcome revelation.

And then Poppy yawned and Caius couldn't help but laugh. She was looking at him, indignant. 'What's so funny?'

He shook his head. He wasn't about to tell her that she was the first woman who'd yawned in his presence and yet he still wanted her.

'I think you've overestimated your energy levels.'

She looked a bit sheepish. 'Maybe.' She looked around wistfully. 'But I'd like to come back.'

Caius curbed the urge to assure her he'd bring her clubbing again, even though the thought of someone else in a place like this with her was momentarily rage-inducing.

He forced himself to say civilly, 'I'm sure you'll be back, but can we go for now?'

'OK.'

Caius took Poppy's hand and told himself the sooner they got back to the apartment and focused on the job of helping this chemistry to burn out, the sooner he could get back to a world where revelations were few and far between and had nothing to do with this woman and her effect on him, and his life.

Back at the apartment, Caius helped Poppy take off the heavy necklace and then pressed a kiss to the back of her neck, feeling her delicate shiver. She said, 'I had a really nice time this evening, Caius. I didn't think I'd enjoy it so much.'

Caius stilled for a moment, because he could agree with her and say he'd enjoyed it too and that that had been unexpected for him, but Caius didn't want to talk because talking would make him think of how it had felt to need to find her distinctive red hair if she wasn't by his side, or how much he'd liked just observing her and her effect on people.

So he just said, 'That's good, I'm glad,' and then he found her zip and pulled it down.

She turned around to face him but she held the dress up. She looked at him and said, 'I think we were good together this evening.'

Caius tensed. 'We were.'

'Do you think you can see a future for us together… once this desire burns out? For the sake of our daughter primarily…but also because maybe we can build on something?'

Caius felt exposed. 'Did I give you the impression that I wanted more?' He'd always been so careful but with Poppy, since that first night, his usual levels of control had gone out of the window.

She bit her lip. 'You know what? Forget I said anything.'

Before Caius could respond to that or really parse out what she was trying to say, she'd pulled down her dress, exposing her breasts, and said, 'Make love to me, Caius, that's all I want.'

Caius weakly pushed aside any misgivings because he wanted her too badly and his blood was on fire.

The ripe curves of her breasts begged for his hands and mouth.

He sat on the edge of the bed and pulled her towards him. 'Now this,' he breathed, 'is what I have wanted all evening.'

He cupped each heavy weight in turn and then lavished the taut peaks with his attention. His mouth, tongue, teeth.

'Oh, God, Caius…my legs, I can't stand…'

Caius pulled her dress down the rest of the way and stood up, letting her get onto the bed. He took off her shoes and pulled down her underwear. She was naked and for a moment he felt humbled by her beauty.

He stripped with indecent haste, making her laugh when he couldn't undo a button and ripped the shirt. He felt feral with the need to join with her and block everything out. Maybe he was the one with the excess hormones?

He came onto the bed and said, 'I need you to be on top, Poppy. I want to see you, riding me.'

He saw her cheeks flush at that suggestion and then she came up and, when he was lying down, straddled him, placing her hot core right *there*, against his erection. Caius groaned. 'You're going to kill me and I'm not even inside you.'

Poppy came up on her knees and reached behind her for him, and this made her back arch and her breasts thrust out. Caius put his hands on her hips and bit his lip when he felt her wrap his cock with her hand and guide him to her entrance.

And then she sank back down, taking him in, so

deep he was seeing stars. She started to move, bending forward slightly, putting her hands on his chest, the movement squeezing her breasts together.

Caius was in the grip of a fever, the sight of Poppy riding him, from her breasts to the fertile swell of her belly, it was the most erotic experience of his life. He could barely keep it together but the second he felt her splinter around him, he let go with a cry of release and when she came forward onto his chest, face buried in his neck, breathing harshly, it was all he could do to rub her back and slide into a sea of blissful oblivion where there was no need to think about what Poppy had tried to say to him. Clearly it hadn't been that important.

At some point he woke, and immediately knew something was wrong. Poppy wasn't in the bed beside him. Had he heard a sound? And then he did hear a sound, like a low moaning.

Caius was up and out of the bed and at the door of the bathroom in a second. He opened the door to find Poppy sitting on the toilet, dressed in a robe. She looked at him and her face was white.

'Caius, I'm bleeding.'

It was all a blur as soon as Caius appeared at the bathroom doorway and took in the situation. Poppy was bundled back onto the bed. Caius pulled on clothes while talking on the phone in curt sentences. Then he was lifting her into his arms and taking her out of the apartment down to the street and into the back of a car and then they were at an emergency room under bright fluorescent lights.

The doctor—who looked as if he'd been called from his bed—did a thorough exam, and a scan, and asked Poppy a million questions and then stood up and pulled his gloves off, saying, 'We'll keep you in overnight for observation but the baby seems well and, as far as I can make out, the bleeding is just some cervical irritation. Did you have sex recently?'

Poppy blushed, very aware of Caius in the room. 'Um, yes, tonight.'

The doctor was totally unfazed. 'OK, well, maybe refrain for a week or two and then keep it to the less energetic end of the scale. Any sign of more bleeding, come straight back in, but, really, I don't think there's anything to worry about. Baby is well.'

The doctor left, a nurse appeared to make sure Poppy was comfortable and the panic was receding. She looked at Caius and realised he was as pale and stricken-looking as she felt.

This evidence that Caius was affected too made Poppy feel emotional. For so long she'd felt on her own, with no one who could share her experience. And she was glad it was Caius. She couldn't help but feel an affinity with him now that she knew so much more about his past.

'Caius, it's OK, the baby is OK.'

He came over and took her hand, shaking his head. 'I'm so sorry, this is my fault.'

'How is it your fault?'

'The sex… I never thought that it could do harm. It was selfish.'

Poppy's mouth opened and shut and then she said, 'It wasn't your fault or mine. It's just a little irritation.'

He took his hand away, his voice heavy with self-recrimination. 'I could have harmed the baby.'

Poppy curled her hand to a fist as if trying to hang onto his warmth. 'No, you couldn't have. Sex during pregnancy is quite normal. The doctor said it was probably just a burst blood vessel!'

He looked at her and his eyes were haunted. 'When I make love to you I forget about everything…maybe I was too rough.'

Poppy's heart turned over. 'You weren't too rough. I was there too, remember? It's the same for me.'

He shook his head. 'I couldn't live with myself if anything happened to the baby.'

Poppy felt both gladdened at the evidence he cared, but also a little ashamed to admit to feeling bereft because obviously she wanted him to care about the baby but she also wanted him to care about her, too.

'She's fine, Caius. You should go and get some rest. I'll be OK.'

He was emphatic. 'No way, I'm staying here.' Poppy remonstrated with him but he was determined.

Eventually she fell asleep with Caius in the bigger chair in the corner of the room, watching her as if she were a parcel that might explode at any moment.

When she woke up next, she saw that Caius was asleep in the chair, head at an awkward angle. He was wearing sweats and a T-shirt. She realised he'd pulled on odd sneakers. And that was when she could no longer stop the surge of emotion. More emotion than she'd felt in her life because she'd spent her whole life damping it down after learning no one wanted her emotion, or love. Not her father and not her mother.

But here, with dawn rising outside and no one else around, Poppy couldn't stop it. She was in love with Caius and all the lessons of her lifetime had come to naught, because she'd just put herself in the worst harm's way when she would suffer the rejection coming her way because Caius didn't feel anything for her.

And she went cold all over to think of how she'd almost exposed herself spectacularly—buoyed up from the evening and the club and everything, she'd actually asked him if there was any possibility they could make it work together…

And he'd looked at her. *'Did I give you the impression that I wanted more?'* No. He had not. She'd just hoped…but clearly any sense of intimacy she'd felt yesterday evening had been rooted purely in the physical. All he'd been concerned with was getting her back into bed.

When she'd expressed she'd like to go clubbing again, he'd very pointedly not included himself in future excursions. She'd noticed that too.

The message was loud and clear. He didn't want emotional involvement. And she got it, he'd been through his own family trauma. Except he'd obviously learnt not to let any vulnerability in. Something she'd failed at.

But maybe where his daugher was concerned, he could love her. And if he did, then Poppy couldn't be selfish and ask for love for her too. If her child could grow up loved by two parents, even if they weren't together, then that would be more than she could hope for. More than she or Caius had had.

At that moment Caius woke up and those eyes seemed to pierce all the way through her. He jumped up. 'Are you OK?'

Her heart ached. 'I'm fine. I just woke up.'

'I'll get the doctor.'

Poppy opened her mouth to protest but he was gone already. This side of attentive, caring Caius was seriously seductive but she had to remember that it was for the baby's sake. Not hers.

The doctor came into the room. 'Well, how did we sleep?'

'Caius, I can walk, you know,' Poppy huffed as Caius scooped her up into his arms from the dining table. They'd been back in the apartment for a week, having been advised to take it easy for a couple of weeks. But there was no indication that anything more sinister was going on. Much to Poppy's relief.

'I'm not taking any chances,' Caius said as he carried her from the dining room up the stairs. A nurse had visited each day to check Poppy and take vitals, et cetera, but Caius had been on hand every moment, hovering like a mother hen, bringing Poppy food, drinks, books, magazines.

As much as she appreciated it, it was beginning to grate on her nerves, as was being in the apartment. 'I need to go for a walk, Caius. I can't go back to bed, it's mid-morning.'

'You need to rest.'

'I'm not an invalid.' Nor was she immune to the fact that Caius's chest felt like warm steel under her and her blood heated in response. The doctor had told them to abstain from sex for this couple of weeks and Poppy was all too aware of how voracious she'd become, acutely aware of the hunger she felt for Caius.

He seemed to be having no such problem, touching her as solicitously as the nurse did. No hint of sexual desire.

He put her down on the side of the bed and stood back. He was wearing dark trousers and a white shirt. He'd been working from the home office, and assistants had been coming and going.

Poppy stood up and said firmly, 'I'm going to put some clothes on and I'm going to go into Central Park. And you should go into the office for a few hours.'

'No.'

Poppy refrained from stamping her foot. 'Caius, I'm going.' She stepped to the side of him and went to the dressing room. He followed her to the door and Poppy ignored him as she shucked off the robe and pulled on underwear, maternity jeans, a bra and a loose shirt.

When she turned around, Caius was red in the face and his jaw was gritted so tight a muscle was pulsing. Her pulse kicked. Was he angry? Or did he want her? If he hadn't lost interest after this little health-scare no-sex interlude, then he soon would. He was a highly sexed guy. And he'd turned her into a highly sexed woman. He'd also made her fall in love with him. Damn him. She slid her feet into a pair of sneakers.

'Don't try to stop me, Caius.'

'I'm coming too.'

Poppy panicked. She realised she needed space from Caius as much as she needed some air and exercise. She already felt as if she was taking up so much of his time. 'You really don't have to. I'll bring my phone. Security will be shadowing me.' Having him fuss over her as though he really cared for the last week, and wanting him, was just about breaking her.

But she wasn't to get any respite. He folded his arms and she recognised that obdurate expression.

'Please, Caius, I just need some air and space.'

An expression crossed his face but it was gone so fast she couldn't interpret it. Eventually some of the tension left his form and he said, 'Fine, but security will be with you, and make sure your phone is on.'

Poppy did a mock salute. 'Aye, aye, sir.'

'Cute,' Caius said, and then, 'Sit down.'

Poppy did, on a chair, and watched, bemused, as Caius bent at her feet and laced up her sneakers. It was just as well—with the bump growing, it was getting harder to do things like bend over.

He stood and put out a hand and she let him pull her up. She was so close to him her belly was pressing against him and after a moment, when Poppy was willing him to just kiss her—so much for her wanting air and space—he moved back and let her go.

'Enjoy your walk.'

Before Poppy could humiliate herself, she left the bedroom and made her way out of the apartment.

CHAPTER TEN

AN HOUR LATER Caius was pacing in his office. Poppy had said she needed *space*. Since when had any woman ever needed space from Caius? Who famously gave so much space to women he'd left a trail of embittered lovers in his wake.

He couldn't win.

He'd sent his staff back to the office because he couldn't focus. He kept imagining Poppy in the park somewhere, doubling over in pain, and had to curb the urge to go and find her.

He knew all he had to do was look at his phone, because he was tracking the security guy who was tracking her.

He would never get that moment out of his head, finding her in the bathroom, her face parchment white. *I'm bleeding.* How Caius had managed to get it together to get her to the hospital was still a blur.

Poppy didn't know that when they'd been examining her he'd almost had a panic attack. A nurse had come and handed him a paper bag. 'Sit down and breathe into this. Your wife is in good hands.'

Caius had taken one look at the bag and he'd shaken

his head. His sister used to have panic attacks, especially whenever she'd see people having arguments, and Caius had learned how to calm her down. He'd arrogantly prided himself on not allowing his emotions to have such a hold over him.

The mere suggestion that *he'd* been having one and the realisation that perhaps he wasn't as immune to dealing with traumatic events as he'd liked to believe had been enough to help him regulate again.

By the time he'd been allowed back into the room to see Poppy, he'd had his reaction under iron control.

And since then he'd used that iron control to clamp down on his libido. He should never have made love to her that night after the event. She'd been tired, and he should have encouraged her to go to bed. Alone.

But he'd wanted her too badly. And he'd needed to block out everything she'd evoked within him.

But then she'd tried to talk to him, asking him if he thought they could have a future together. He could remember the feeling of exposure. The immediate need to shut it down to avert a fight-or-flight response clawing up from his gut.

But before it could take hold, Poppy had taken his lead and closed it down and asked him to make love to her and Caius had never been so eager to selfishly pursue his own pleasure and that was what had almost—He stopped pacing and went cold again. No wonder she wanted space.

Clearly he shouldn't be around her. She didn't even seem to be all that aware of him, she'd just stripped off in front of him to change and he'd almost exploded at the sight of her naked body with that perfect bump and her high full breasts, blue veins visible under the skin.

Maybe he was freaking her out because she sensed his desire and she was more focused on keeping the baby safe. From him. Caius knew he was being irrational, but wanting Poppy and hating himself for believing he might have harmed her and the baby was tangling him up in knots.

He'd almost had a panic attack. Evidence that emotions were high, and not a good sign. Emotions spelled lack of control and chaos and weakness and the kind of spiralling Caius was experiencing now. He had to protect Poppy from that, from himself.

Since when had he forgotten that he'd gone into this marriage with a view to getting out as soon as possible? Since when had he begun to believe that he belonged?

Since when had the anatomy of his life changed so much that he'd forgotten the very basic rule of never allowing anyone to come too close? He had to remember the bottom line here, which was a marriage of convenience to give their baby legitimacy and then, once the baby was born and they'd laid down ground rules for Caius to have a relationship with his daughter, they could get on with separate lives.

When Poppy got back to the apartment, she felt so much better. Fresh air and exercise. It was the first proper chance she'd had to think about things since her revelation in the hospital. The revelation that she loved Caius. And the fact that rejection—the thing she'd feared all her life—was inevitable.

She had to be careful not to forget that, because Caius in caring mode was seriously seductive. But it was concern for the baby, not her. Oh, she didn't doubt he cared for her—but only as the mother of his child.

Without sex muddying the waters, it was clear Caius had no problem keeping his distance. And that really shouldn't be a problem because the most important thing was that he was so accepting of his baby daughter. More than accepting.

And the prospect of Caius wanting to be a very committed parent was something Poppy had hoped for but figured wouldn't happen.

Now, it was a distinct possibility.

But, selfishly, the thought of him deciding to commit to this relationship for the sake of their daughter terrified Poppy.

She'd spent her life with someone who had rejected her on a daily basis. Who hadn't loved her. She couldn't do it again. It had reduced her to a shell of herself. Stripped her confidence. She wouldn't let her daughter watch that happen. Maybe Caius was so invested in his child now that he would fight to be in her life on a permanent basis?

She needed to know what Caius intended so she could be prepared.

She was so preoccupied that she didn't notice that the apartment was quiet. No sounds coming from Caius's office. She felt an ominous prickling skate over her skin, as if something seismic had happened but she had no idea what.

She almost jumped out of her skin when one of the

nurses appeared in the doorway. The young woman apologised and said, 'Mr Mansur told me to let you know that he's taken your advice to go into the office and he'll call you later.'

'OK, thank you.' Poppy forced a smile, absorbing this news. This was a good thing. He'd taken her suggestion on board. So why did she feel suddenly bereft that her constant Caius Nightingale wasn't here? Although he wasn't leaving her alone.

The nurse said now, 'Maybe we should check you over. Mr Mansur said you'd been out for a walk? How are you feeling?'

Poppy fought not to roll her eyes. Caius might not be here but he was making sure she was being monitored at all times. Suddenly she didn't want space any more, she wanted Caius, even if she couldn't have him, and if he wouldn't touch her.

She was losing it. She meekly went with the nurse and allowed the woman to persuade her to take a rest.

Much later that night, when Caius came back, he was feeling slightly less volatile. Until he walked in and saw the figure of Poppy lying on the couch in the den area.

The nurse hovered in the door and whispered, 'She was watching a movie and fell asleep. I thought I'd leave her.'

Caius nodded and said, 'Thanks, you can retire for the night.'

She left and Caius looked at Poppy on the couch. Her vibrant hair was fanned out around her head and her features were at rest.

His chest tightened. She was so beautiful. And unexpected. And disturbing to his equilibrium. He'd spent many selfish years ignoring the emptiness inside him, the feeling of worthlessness, but for the first time in his life, these past few months, he'd felt whole.

She might believe that they could build a future together, but he did not deserve to use Poppy to feel good about himself. And his daughter deserved better than a father who hadn't the first clue about how to be a father. But it was too late to change that. All he could do was go by Poppy's guidance and try to do no harm.

He thought of Poppy waking and those green eyes seeing into his soul where this volatile mix was barely under control.

He scooped her up into his arms and she made a little sound but didn't wake. Caius carried her up the stairs and gritted his jaw against how she felt in his arms. Warm and soft and fragrant.

When he put her down on the bed, the blanket the nurse had placed over her slipped down and all Caius could do was look and curse silently. She was wearing a loose T-shirt and it had slipped down, revealing the upper slope of her breast.

His blood roared and he shook with the effort it took not to rouse her and have her open her arms to him. And it wasn't just the physical release he needed, it was so much more. He wanted her to take his jagged edges and make them smooth.

He took a step back. And that was why he had to let her go, before he trapped her in a cage of his needs and desires, using her to fool himself into thinking he was a good person, who deserved the kind of uncomplicated things most people took for granted. Things like *love* and *hope*. Redemption. Caius smiled mirthlessly at the quaint notion.

'Are you sure you're feeling up to this?' Caius asked.

'Yes,' Poppy responded, feeling out of sorts and irritable. And then more out of sorts for feeling grumpy. It wasn't Caius's fault. For the past few days, since she'd taken that walk, he'd been the absolute epitome of kindness, generosity and solicitude.

When he'd been around. But he'd barely been around.

He'd been at the office or he'd taken business dinners and meetings, late. Poppy had tried to stay up one night to catch him to talk to him but she'd woken in her bed, to find the night nurse sitting outside her room reading a book with a night light.

She knew the night nurse couldn't have carried her to bed, so it had to have been Caius.

But as of today the doctor had given her the all-clear and now she was alone with Caius, finally. Well, in the back of a chauffeur-driven SUV, but she couldn't concentrate because Caius was dressed for the polo match and he was wearing jodhpurs, a polo shirt and boots. And all she wanted to do was climb onto his lap and cleave herself to him.

But maybe this was the only chance she'd get to speak to him, so she turned towards him and said, 'Caius, there's something we should probably—'

But his phone rang and, with an apologetic grimace, he said, 'That's my assistant, sorry, I have to take it.'

That call was followed by another call, and another, and soon they were turning into the lush green ground of the polo club on Long Island. And then Poppy was being whisked off to the VIP hospitality area while Caius went to join his team.

Poppy gave up the notion she'd speak to him now and settled in for the afternoon of watching her first polo game. It was mesmerising. The horses were sleek and lean and the men—one of whom was another European prince she recognised—were honed and muscular.

None more so than Caius. She couldn't take her eyes off him. He moved with the horse as one. She'd known he was a good horseman after seeing him in Valdere, but here, he was part of the horse, moving so fast sometimes he was a blur.

At one point, during a break, she saw him laughing, head thrown back, surrounded by teammates. He looked really happy. He was back in his milieu. Maybe the distance he'd been imposing was the start of him reintegrating with his old life.

Maybe she had it all wrong and he had no intention of wanting to spend more time with his daughter than he'd already committed to?

Maybe the lack of sex had made him see what he was missing. Maybe he just didn't want her any more and was avoiding having to reject her if she came onto him? Poppy's head hurt with all the *maybes*.

When his team had won and the trophy was to be

presented, one of the officials came up to Poppy and said, 'Queen Poppy, you must do us the honour of presenting the trophy.'

Poppy couldn't very well refuse but she was uberconscious of herself as she made her way to the little podium. She was wearing a light blue wrap dress that flattered her curves and matching wedge sandals. Hair pulled back into a loose chignon. But she hated the little prick of insecurity that she cut an ungainly figure.

Caius came and met her at the podium and held out a hand to help her up the steps. She savoured the physical contact in spite of all of the unknowns and her senses went into overdrive when she registered the smell of earthy, sweaty male. His shirt was soaked and his jodhpurs were moulded to his powerful thighs. Hair damp and curling at his neck. Streaks of muck on his face.

Poppy almost forgot what she had to do, she was so overcome with piercing lust. But somehow she managed to hand over the trophy without dropping it and Caius pulled her closer, saying sotto voce, 'We should kiss.'

Something lanced her that he was saying that instead of just doing it. The chasm between them yawned wide open. 'It's OK, Caius, you can kiss me.'

He did, but it was an all too brief brush across the lips. Nevertheless it ignited every nerve-ending. Poppy could feel herself sweating and she knew it wasn't the heat. She wanted to go to some private place with Caius exactly as he was and have him make love to her, hard and fast and—

'I'll just shower and change and then we'll go, OK?'

She nodded abruptly, terrified she'd do something crazy like grab his shirt and beg him to make love to her.

Poppy didn't try to talk to Caius on the way back to the apartment because of the driver and because, truthfully, she wasn't sure what to even say, but when they walked back in the door Poppy turned to him before he could escape again. 'We should talk, Caius. You can't keep avoiding me for ever.'

He looked wary. 'I wanted to give you space.'

Poppy walked into the main living room and kicked off her wedges. She turned around. 'I needed space on that one day, to go for a walk, not for you to go out of your way to treat me like I've had the plague.'

'That wasn't my intention.'

'What's going on, Caius? You know the doctor has said everything is OK. It was nothing serious. You don't have to keep your distance in case you harm me, or the baby.' She wasn't quite ready to spell out how much she wanted him, not when he was being so distant.

And then before he could say anything she blurted out, 'You looked happy today, Caius. Happier than I've seen you before.'

Caius thought of that moment with his friends on the polo pitch. He hadn't been happy, not really. He'd been happy to see Poppy among the crowd and then she'd looked at him and for some reason he'd needed her to think he was happy so he'd laughed, but the emptiness inside had mocked him. Because this charade was over.

Today he'd seen a glimpse of the world he'd left behind, hedonistic and frantic, and he'd felt no remorse or hunger for it.

He'd tried to pretend he could be part of Poppy's world, but he couldn't, because this wasn't the serene, *boring*, arranged marriage he'd always envisaged for himself. It was anything but serene and boring. It was alive and electric and full of desires that terrified him with their intensity.

Today, when she'd come up onto the stage to give him the trophy, he'd wanted to rip her dress open and feast on her and then bury himself so deep inside her he'd never get lost again. And he'd wanted to do that to sate the beast inside him, but also, and more disturbingly, so that he could ignore the way she made him feel. He had an awful suspicion he needed her for his very survival.

The fact that he'd lost his bearings so completely and had blindly put himself at risk of needing someone with an emotional intensity he'd avoided his whole life was…absolutely terrifying. It spelled chaos and destruction.

He said, 'I've been playing make-believe, Poppy. Trying to make-believe that this can work.'

Poppy stood before him and a part of him marvelled at her regal grace. She was a queen and she was every inch a queen now. A fertile goddess. And she deserved more than a man who wasn't worthy of her.

She frowned now. 'What are you talking about?'

'I'm talking about the fact that the honeymoon is over. We've given everyone a show and now we can get on with our original plan, which was to appear together for occasions and maintain our separate lives.'

'You're still blaming yourself for the baby.'

Caius shook his head even as that image of Poppy's pale, stricken face came into his mind. 'No, I know it wasn't my fault. Our fault.' But he had used sex to avoid dealing with his emotions and he could never forgive himself if that was what had led to the scare.

He said, 'Since being back in New York, I've realised how much work I have to do here.'

'What about our daughter?' Poppy's voice sounded a little faint.

Caius had a flashback to when Poppy had told him she was pregnant in this very room, and it nearly felled him to think of all that had happened in the meantime.

'I will be in her life, as much as I can be, but she will be better off with you, in Valdere.' Before he could stop it, Caius had a vision of a little girl with dark red hair, running to him, and it filled him with an almost giddy feeling. He shut it down. He did not know the first thing about being a father and he did not have the emotional skills to be able to deal with a daughter. The prospect that he would disappoint her was far greater than any fantasy alternative.

'You need to go back to Valdere, Poppy.'

Poppy wasn't sure how she was still standing. She hated Caius in that moment. Because he was rejecting her with the cold precision of a knife sliding through her ribs. Straight to the heart.

And she shouldn't be surprised, because she had

known. Because even if he hadn't shut down her attempt to ask him if he saw a future for them, from the very start—that day on the hill on the lake island—he'd laid out how it would be. Humiliation crawled over her skin.

He no longer even wanted her.

She desperately needed to claw back any sense of control she could. 'You originally only wanted to be married for a year.'

His face looked stark, stripped of all emotion. 'Yes.'

'I'll change the marriage agreement. I think a year is more than enough. It'll be better for the baby not to have any memory of a marriage that is a charade.' Great, now she was calling their daughter *the baby.* But she couldn't bring herself to say *daughter* in front of him. All the dreams she'd dared to dream of them being a family, finding some sort of happiness against the odds, mocked her viciously now.

'If that's what you want.'

'It is. We can liaise about any future requirements to meet through our teams.'

Before Poppy's veneer of ice could crack she turned and went to the door. As she put her hand on the knob Caius said from behind her, 'Poppy, wait.'

But she didn't want to hear it. Was he going to apologise? The thought made her insides curdle. She just said, 'Goodnight, Caius.' And left.

The following morning Poppy was on a private jet back to Valdere, along with a doctor and nurse. Caius had insisted. As if he cared. He might still care about the baby, but he'd never cared for her. He'd wanted her, yes, and he'd just seduced her into thinking it was more with his well-worn seduction routine. But the man she'd seen at the polo match—vibrant and surrounded by his peers? That had been the old Caius Mansur de Roche and he was obviously eager to get back to what he did best.

She would never forgive him, or herself, for allowing him to sneak so deep under her skin that he could inflict maximum damage.

Her daughter kicked under her ribs and Poppy put a hand over her bump. All she could do now was get on with the job of running her country and ensure that, above all, Caius didn't hurt their daughter.

She somehow managed to keep a lid on the seething, roiling emotions threatening to rise up and pull her down, but she couldn't hold it in when she saw Stephen waiting for her. He managed to get her into the back of a car before anyone saw her distress but, through a waterfall of tears, she said, 'I've been so stupid.'

He shook his head, and hugged her and pulled back and said, 'No, sweetie, you've just been human and fallen in love.'

It wasn't much comfort to hear that, in spite of being a queen, she was still at the mercy of very basic human weaknesses. As if she hadn't known that already.

A week after Poppy had left, Caius found himself in the dressing room of his apartment. All of the clothes that had been installed for Poppy were still hanging up. He spied the blue dress she'd worn to the polo match and gathered it up, holding it to his face, breathing in her scent.

He wasn't sure how much time passed but when he caught sight of himself in the mirror, for a second he thought someone else was in the room. He blinked and realised it was himself. In sweats and a creased T-shirt, beard unkempt, hair wild. Eyes wilder.

He hadn't been sleeping. He'd been having nightmares. All featuring various versions of Poppy looking at him with horror and disdain if he tried to come close to her.

But last night, he'd dreamt of his daughter. Of holding out his arms to her and of her turning away and running to Poppy, crying.

Caius made his way down to the drinks cabinet and poured himself a shot of whiskey, throwing it back. He didn't need to be Sigmund Freud to interpret that. It was pathetically obvious.

'Caius?'

Was he hearing things? He turned around and it took a second for him to realise who he was looking at.

'Cassie?'

His beautiful blonde sister came towards him with concern on her face. 'Caius, what's going on? You were supposed to have a meeting with Ares today while we're in New York and you never showed and we couldn't contact you.'

She looked around. 'Where's Poppy?'

'I sent her home.' Caius's voice was harsh. It had to be, or it would crack under the strain of the emotions in his gut.

Cassie looked at him and took it in. And saw. 'Oh, Caius, what have you done?'

Ten days, Poppy thought to herself. It had only been ten days and she could barely remember what it had been like to feel…not in pain. Emotional pain. She cursed Caius again. His rejection had made anything she'd experienced with her father look like a walk in the park.

She let the groom help her put the saddle on the horse. She was aware of the young man glancing at her a little fearfully, no doubt put off by her stony expression. She had to force herself to smile at him when he'd finished tacking up the horse.

And then she noticed his eyes flicker to something behind her and widen, and he suddenly melted away. Poppy turned around and everything in her seemed to plummet to the ground—blood, heart, stomach—when she saw who it was.

'Caius.' She had to say his name. She wasn't sure if she was hallucinating. Maybe he'd migrated from her fevered dreams to daytime hallucinations.

'Poppy.'

His deep voice hit her right in the solar plexus and reverberated like ripples on a pond, igniting nerve-endings. Igniting her anger.

'Does Stephen know you're here?'

He nodded. 'I just saw him.'

And Stephen wasn't here trying to stop Caius from talking to her. A nugget that had significance but not the kind of significance that Poppy wanted to even think about. She was going to fire Stephen.

'What do you want, Caius? I told you any discussions would be between our teams.'

'I want to talk to you…to try to explain…what happened in New York.'

Poppy opened her eyes wide. 'Nothing happened in New York. I came home and you were getting back to your life.'

Poppy turned to the horse and put her foot in the stirrup. She prayed she wouldn't look like some ungainly baby elephant as she swung her leg over the horse's back, but she managed to get into the saddle without making a spectacle of herself. And it was satisfying to look down on Caius, who she noticed now was wearing jeans and a loose shirt.

He looked somehow…diminished though. As if the stuffing had been knocked out of him. Some vital spark dulled. She pushed down the urge to ask him if he was OK.

'I'm going for a ride, Caius. Please see yourself out of the palace.' She turned the horse to head out of the stableyard and only vaguely heard a curse behind her. She didn't care. She was shaking now. Shaking with shock and adrenalin and something much more awful. *Hope.*

She was along the trail when she heard the sound of another horse behind her. She didn't turn around. She knew it was him. They stayed like that for a while, Caius behind her, saying nothing, until they came to a clearing with a small pool. It was warm. Poppy knew the horses needed to rest and drink water.

She got off her horse and tied it off to a tree. And finally looked at Caius, who was securing his horse.

She faced him, hands on her hips. 'Why are you following me, Caius?'

'I'm sorry, Poppy, I never wanted to hurt you.'

Oh, God, he was here because he felt sorry for her. Poppy hitched up her chin. 'Don't be ridiculous, Caius. In order to hurt me I'd have to have feelings for you and I couldn't care less.' The baby kicked her. Poppy ignored it. The little traitor.

'Well, that's good, because you shouldn't care for me at all, because I have nothing to offer you except myself and that is a man who has avoided having to engage with anything emotional his entire life for fear of becoming his parents.

'And,' he went on, 'for fear of letting anyone close enough to see that underneath all the smoke and mirrors was just an empty existence devoid of any meaning. My coronation day was the worst. I'd never felt like a bigger fraud.'

Poppy's hands dropped from her hips, anger draining away. 'Caius…you're not a fraud.'

He smiled but it was sad. 'You knew I was a fraud. You called me one, remember?'

But before Poppy could protest that she hadn't meant it like that, he was saying, 'But I don't feel like a fraud when I'm with you. I feel real. Worth something, just from the way you look at me, like you see something no one else ever has…except maybe Cassie. She came to see me in New York.'

'Cassie?'

He nodded. 'She knows…how it was for us. She knew I'd done something to push you away because it's hard for us to believe that we can find the kind of happiness we never experienced.'

Poppy swallowed. He was saying a lot but it still didn't mean… 'Why are you here, Caius?'

'Because there's nowhere else I want to be,' he said simply. 'Even before we had the scare with the baby, I knew I was fighting a losing battle trying to keep a lid on my emotions. You tried to talk to me about a future, that night…the night of the event, and I pretended I didn't know what you were talking about, but of course I did, but I couldn't even give such a suggestion air, because I would have had to admit I wanted more too, and I wasn't ready to do that…'

His mouth thinned in self-disgust. 'So I made love to you…any excuse to avoid opening up, and I wanted you so much… I was trying to fool myself that the sex was divorced from my emotions but of course it wasn't…but then you—' Caius stopped talking, going pale.

Poppy's insides twisted. 'Caius, you know it wasn't the sex.'

He swallowed visibly. 'Maybe I'll fully believe that one day but—'

Poppy put up her hand. 'Stop, right there.' She walked towards Caius, stopping a couple of feet away. 'You have to stop blaming yourself for something that had nothing to do with us having sex, or how much we want each other.'

Caius's eyes widened. 'You just said how much we want each other.'

'I never stopped wanting you, Caius. I felt crazy that day at the polo, I wanted you so badly. But you could barely touch me.'

He shook his head. 'I never stopped wanting you, Poppy. I will never stop wanting you. But it scares me, the depth of desire I feel, like it'll be destructive.'

'How can something that feels so good be destructive?'

'Because the only passion I ever saw was dark, possessive, jealous and ruinous.'

'That wasn't passion, Caius, that was two broken people hurting each other.'

'I think I know that… It's just taken me a while to understand it because I never had to think about it before, until I met you and suddenly I was wanting and feeling so much and…terrified to let it out. I didn't know how to handle it.'

Poppy said, 'I'm scared too, Caius, scared of rejection and of everyone around me ignoring me and not seeing me because I'm not worth anything.'

'I see you, Poppy, and you are worth everything.'

Somehow, without even knowing they'd moved, Poppy was in Caius's arms, their gazes locked onto one another.

He said, 'I'm so sorry for pushing you away…for being such a coward that I had to reject you.'

'You're not a coward. You are worth so much, Caius. You are good and full of integrity and you make me feel like I can do anything.'

He smiled and tucked a wayward hair behind her ear. 'You can, you're magnificent.'

Feeling dreamy, Poppy said, 'You still haven't told me why you're here.'

'Because I wanted to tell you that I don't want a year, or five years, I want a lifetime. I want to be your consort, your husband, your lover, and I want to try and be a father to our daughter even though I haven't a clue what to do. I just knew it would kill me if I was some sort of stranger to her. I want to fight to prove I'm worthy of you, and her.'

Poppy lifted his hand and kissed it and looked up at him. 'You will be an amazing father—you've already been a father to your sister but you don't even recognise it.'

She went on, 'There's just one thing missing.'

'What?' Caius looked a little frantic.

'Do you love me, Caius?'

An intensity suffused his face, his eyes blindingly blue. 'Poppy, what I feel for you doesn't even come close to any definition of love I've ever heard. You consume me. I want you. I need you. I don't ever want to take my eyes off you…and the idea that we've created something, someone, that's an extension of you…'

Caius put a shaking hand to his chest. 'I feel so full, I don't know where to put it. If that's love, then, yes… I love you.'

It was all she needed to hear. Poppy mentally rehired Stephen and reached up, winding her arms tight around Caius's neck, her belly pressed against him. Her vision was blurry. 'Oh, Caius, you don't have to put it anywhere except let it out, share it with me… I love you so much.' She said shakily, 'I thought you were gone, back to your life…'

He shuddered in her arms. 'No way, that was such an empty existence. Do you really mean it, Poppy? You love me?'

She nodded. 'More than anything. Now will you please make love to me before I explode because I've missed you so much?'

Caius looked worried and Poppy said, 'Caius Mansur, if you don't kiss me and make love to me right here, right now, I'll have you deported.'

He smiled. 'I guess if we're gentle it'll be OK.'

Poppy pressed her mouth to his and he kissed her back, she pulled away and started to strip off, desperate to feel Caius where she needed him most, pulling him down onto the ground and opening her body to him. There was no foreplay, Caius joined his body to hers and all talk of being gentle went out the window as the fire rose up around them and consumed them both, leaving them in a state of shattered bliss just minutes later.

Caius came up on one elbow and looked down at the woman he adored more than his own life. She looked drowsy and sated and pink and so beautiful. And she was his, and he was hers. And when she looked at him now and saw right into him, he felt peace. He would never hide again. He knew that he might never be worthy of her but he would do his damnedest to fight to be. For the rest of their lives.

EPILOGUE

Two years later, Sadat Sur Mer, The Palace

'You see, it's all about the way you hold her. If you scoop her up like this and let her rest on her front, along your forearm, it means that she's not fighting her wind, she's more comfortable.'

Ares gently bounced Bella, one of his one-month-old twin girls, on his arm, the way Caius was demonstrating with her twin, Calli. Both babies certainly seemed content.

'Where did you learn this?' Ares asked suspiciously.

Caius tapped his nose. 'If I told you I'd have to kill you.'

Ares rolled his eyes.

Just then their wives appeared on the veranda, which was strewn with rugs, cushions and various baby paraphernalia. A table was set up for lunch nearby.

Caius's gaze feasted on Poppy. She was six months pregnant, with their second baby, and she carried their still-sleepy toddler daughter on one hip. Giulia had dark red hair like her mother and Caius's blue eyes. Exactly as he'd imagined. She saw him and put out her arms. 'Papa.'

Cassie came and expertly scooped up her baby and Poppy transferred Giulia to Caius with a rueful smile, saying, 'Such a daddy's girl.' Caius smirked but behind the smirk was genuine emotion. He could have so easily let fear consume him and never have known this depth of love and feeling.

The little girl snuggled close and put her thumb in her mouth, still half asleep. Caius knew it wouldn't last long, she'd soon be tearing around the place giving him a million heart attacks a minute with her fearless antics.

Cassie sounded amused. 'Caius, were you showing Ares your baby-whispering skills again?'

Poppy laughed and Caius grumbled at their teasing. 'What? The methods work!'

They settled down to lunch, a semi-chaotic affair with babies being passed around, fed, winded, and Giulia coming fully awake and demanding attention, but, in the midst of it all, Caius and Poppy shared a look that held the wealth of everything they felt and didn't need to say.

It didn't go unnoticed however. When the babies were both down in the twin bassinet, sleeping, Ares scooped up Giulia and said, 'Want to come and play hide and seek?'

'Babababa!' she squealed, her version of *yes*. And then he looked at Caius and Poppy and said, 'I would respectfully suggest that you two take advantage of this to go take your own nap. Those looks are getting a little too R-rated.'

Cassie laughed and Caius glared at Ares but Poppy was already dragging him out of his seat and into the palace and about an hour later, when they had both not taken a nap but were dozing in the sated aftermath, they could hear Giulia somewhere outside saying, 'More, more!'

Poppy chuckled. 'It sounds like we need to go rescue someone.'

Caius put an arm around Poppy, pulling her back against him, his hand spread across the swell of her belly. She sucked in an audible breath when she felt his erection and Caius said, 'Maybe just a few more minutes?'

Poppy turned to him and smiled. 'Maybe for ever.'

'For ever it is.' He covered her mouth with his and they moved together, committing to each other over and over again. For ever.

* * * * *

Did you fall in love with
Unmasking His Pregnant Queen*? Then make sure to check out the previous instalment in the Royal House of Sadat duet,*
Bodyguard's Royal Temptation.
In the meantime, explore these other stories by Abby Green!

The Heir Dilemma
On His Bride's Terms
Rush to the Altar
Billion-Dollar Baby Shock
Bride of Betrayal

Available now!